OLD SOLDIERS NEVER LAUGH

AND OTHER STORIES

BY

LIEUTENANT-COLONEL W.A. LEAVEY (RET'D)

EDITED BY KAREN HANN

INTRODUCTION BY KAREN HANN

Lammi
Publishing Inc.

Published by Lammi Publishing, Inc. Headquartered in Coaldale, Alberta, Canada. http://lammipublishing.ca

Cover image credit: Alexander Young-Jackson/Canada/Canadian War Museum/19710261-0187

Text and content editing by Karen Hann.

Cover design by Paul Hewitt Battlefield Design, UK. Book layout by www.ebooklaunch.com

Contents

INTRODUCTION

I've had the pleasure of working with Lieutenant Colonel (ret'd) W.A. Leavey (Bill to us) for the five years he's been contributing to Lammi Publishing. From the first piece of work he sent us, I was struck by his wit, his intelligence, his honour, his devotion to the military and his duty, and his uncanny ability to find both humour and wisdom in seemingly ordinary circumstances.

Old Soldiers Never Laugh is the first short story collection that Bill will publish with us. Featuring both fiction and creative nonfiction, this text shows us much of what makes him tick as a human being, as a family man, as a retired soldier, as a humourist, as an absurdist, and as an observer of the human condition.

The stories in this collection range widely. In Part 1, we delve into the eccentricities of Bill's rather... eclectic family in the creative nonfiction tales of "It's All Relative." Part 2, entitled "Everyday People" continues to showcase Bill's unique way of capturing the magic of ordinary existence in a series of fictional stories that bring to humorous life the follies and foibles of a range of characters, from an ambitious clothier to a young military cadet to an army housewife and others. The third part ("A World with Whimsy") brings us a bit absurd realism, as Bill delves into the fantastical with two rather unique tales of what might very well happen to everyday folks if a real bit of magic was tossed into the works. Finally, in Part 4, "Moments that Made Me Myself," we move back into creative nonfiction as Bill shares with us some of the more profound (and hilarious) occasions of his own life that have shaped him into the man he is today, including coping with the foibles of ageing, managing the romantic expectations of a commercialized holiday, and confronting his own mental health.

In this collection, we travel across the great nation of Canada, from a fishing town in Nova Scotia to the British Columbia coast, from a mental health hospital in Manitoba to a television studio in Kingston. We encounter such venerable Canadian institutions as the Maple Leaf Gardens and Fort Henry. We experience moments as public (and rare) as an NHL win for the Leafs and moments as private and commonplace as the bickering between a long-wed couple seeking to buy a new oven.

So read on and laugh alongside an old soldier as he shows us how the funniest and most profound moments of life happen on the ordinary days, when we least expect it.

Karen Hann
Editor, Lammi Publishing

Dedication

I wish to dedicate this book of stories to my mother and father Phyllis and Albert Leavey whose DNA endowed me with my satiric and salubrious and sometimes scatological sense of humour.

Part 1

It's All Relative

ZEB AND FANNY

My extended family includes almost 300 relatives if you count cousins, siblings, parents, grandparents, uncles, and aunts. And that doesn't include outlaws, as I refer to them (most would call them in-laws, but my family's special). That would probably double the number. I can't walk around my hometown for ten minutes without running into a relative, in-law, outlaw, or someone else connected to me by blood or special license. This, of course, gives me great grist for my mill of writing family stories. The most memorable stories are, of course the funny ones.

Uncle Zeb and Aunt Fanny were a peculiar pair if there ever was one. Zeb was cantankerous and irascible at best, but Fanny was just plain ornery and bellicose. Many of the siblings would often repeat that Fanny's mouth had the best right hook in the family. Zeb's favourite saying was that "Love is blind, and marriage is an institution. Who wants to go to an institution for the blind?"

Zeb's brother Ben would often opine, with a chuckle, that his brother must have had the patience of a Maple Leaf's fan to put up with Fanny all those years. In retort, Fanny's sister Joyce, (the one who was still talking to her) would quip whenever she had the chance that "Zeb is like a fine wine—he gets better with age and he should be locked in the cellar."

When two such souls decide to spend their lives together, quiet marital harmony isn't in the picture. Their fights were legendary. Tales of their latest dustup were regularly told during breakfast the local diner. Zeb and Fanny weren't particular about who might witness their shenanigans, be it family, neighbours, or even strangers. It became sort of a rite of passage in town for newcomers to see a Zeb and Fanny row. You weren't really a settled citizen until you'd experienced that.

Now, there were a few good things about their marriage. For example, they never did manage to have children. It seemed that they were always too mad at each other to sleep together long enough to procreate.

Perhaps that was unfortunate for them. For the world in general, that was a blessing. Any offspring that inherited a combination of Zeb and Fanny's characteristics and personalities (DNA in modern parlance) was likely to be too terrifying to contemplate. Besides, Fanny lamented, Zeb was a sprinter when it came to sex. He was like Ben Johnson, real fast when he was full of drugs.

There may have been reasons for Fanny's ever-tense, unsatisfied demeanour.

Zeb spoke no more fondly of his wife. "Fanny and I never go to bed mad; we stay up until the problem is resolved. Last winter we didn't get to sleep till the end of February."

Little sleep, less sex... no small wonder they were an irascible pair.

How they ever got together in the first place, and put up with each other for so long, was one of those eternal mysteries within the family lore where nobody'd ever know the real answer. Rumours ran the gamut from having got caught with their pants down in the icehouse by the parish priest to Zeb having lost a bet somewhere to the two of them sharing a bottle of Old Man Greeber's hooch and waking up married. Someone asked at their thirty-fifth anniversary how they'd stayed together all those years, and both Zeb and Fanny agreed that it was because they were so compatible—they both loved to fight!

And yes, that particular party ended up with Fanny hurling a piece of vanilla buttercream cake at Zeb's laughing face.

Anyway, like most close family relations, there's a favourite story that's been making the rounds for as long as I can remember. It seems that Zeb and Fanny, (Fanny and Zeb, as Fanny would always insist) were on their way to a party. It was a rare event, for them to go out in public together, especially since the theme of the fest was family unity and bliss. They were seldom invited more than once because they always caused an outrageous scene of some sort (Greeber, Jr. never did get that bannister properly fixed), but the host obviously did not know them, well—at all. I think they must've been newcomers to town.

This time however, disaster struck before they even got out the door.

Fanny got the zipper to her brand-new cocktail dress hopelessly snagged. In desperation, because the time was short, and since there was no alternative, she reluctantly sought her husband's assistance. Since all of Zeb's attempts at chivalry to date had been unmitigated failures, he less than enthusiastically agreed to help her. Zeb grabbed the zipper and fiddled with it for a while, but it wouldn't budge. And, like always, Zeb had a good idea of how to fix the problem with the least muss and fuss. He ran out to the garage and returned with a shiny pair of pliers. After he had the zipper tongue securely squeezed in the jaws of the pliers, he reefed at it several times twisting the pliers. Finally, in frustration, he pulled it violently down. A rasping, renting, tearing sound was followed immediately by a savage berating from my aunt.

"I never should have let you touch it!" she roared.

The neighbours claim it went on for hours. They learned a fair bit. Fanny had searched for months to find that particular garment. It had cost over two hundred dollars, the money she'd saved by switching to home perms for a full year. She'd gone to the city to buy it, and no other woman in town would have one like it. She was supposed to be the talk of the town for her fine fashion. It was the most beautiful thing she'd ever had, and he'd gone and ruined it. He was an idiot. He couldn't do anything right. He did it on purpose, just to ruin her dress and ruin her night, just like he'd ruined everything else in her life.

But, back to the zipper incident. Most of the neighbours were out on their porches by now, beers in hand, enjoying that ubiquitous 'Zeb and Fanny Show' that aired with more steady regularity than the evening news. It was generally far more entertaining.

"Sorry Love," Zeb said, trying desperately to feign remorse, with obvious limited success. He couldn't stop laughing. That was one of his unfortunate afflictions. Big brother Jim was the same. Family trait, I think, right down to the genes.

Fanny continued to rage.

Objects were thrown. The neighbours couldn't agree amongst themselves exactly what they were... the stories range from Fanny's purse to her shoe to the front grill of a '66 Chevy. As Fanny's aim was terrible (or maybe she didn't want to actually injure her husband), nothing actually hit Zeb on this occasion.

Through the whole tirade, the beleaguered Zeb stood helplessly with a wrinkled smile on his face and a twisted piece of zipper attached by hanging threads to a tattered piece of cloth held limply in his hand.

They never did get to that party. But the whole neighbourhood got to sit on their porches and enjoy some live entertainment that was peppered with far more obscenities than they could find on the television before ten at night.

Zeb knew better than to gloat too much. Fanny could be quite vindictive, even Machiavellian, when she set her mind to it. And she had obviously set her mind to it—with alacrity. Zeb knew her well; she would get him. It was just a matter of time. Zeb waited stoically, but fearfully for the guillotine to drop with Fanny as the smiling executioner. But after some more shrieking and throwing, she just stomped off inside, leaving their audience rather disappointed they didn't get to see her pouring out his homemade hooch (Old Man Greeber's recipe).

Eventually, Zeb decided he'd better curry a bit of favour and perhaps make up for his poor decision. Their twenty-fifth wedding anniversary was coming up.

On advice from big brother Jim, who was equally prone to faux pas with his own wife and women in general, Zeb schemed to get some nice flowers for Fanny to celebrate the occasion. Jim knew the director at the local funeral parlor, and he talked him into giving Zeb a nice big, slightly used, bouquet of white roses for free. Rather than the usual baby's breath, this particular bouquet had ranunculus, ruscus, and salal tips, an unusual combination for the local floral shop. This was a major triumph for Zeb, since he was by nature, like his big brother, a very cautious steward of his cash. If were being blunt about it, he was bloody tightfisted. It was quite a thing around town, for the various business owners, to be able to claim that they'd sold Jim or Zeb something at full price.

Big brother Jim once bought his wife Jenny a frying pan and an iron for Christmas presents (the same Christmas). When he bought her the exact same blender, three years in a row, Aunt Jenny forbade him to buy her another Christmas gift on pain of banishment from their house. That was, in the end, Jim's plan all along, to be relieved of the burden of purchasing gifts.

That's who was coaching Zeb in matters of marital bliss.

But, Zeb mused, he'd get brownie points from Fanny for the flowers and didn't have to pay for them. This was truly win-win.

There was, of course, one small flaw in all of this.

The funeral people forgot to take out the sympathy card from the bouquet, which read "In deepest sympathy for your loss."

Though Zeb wasn't always the quick-thinking sort, he tried to pass it off as an apology for her destroyed dress, that he now understood the enormity of her loss.

Maybe Fanny might have bought it had she not been at the exact funeral where that bouquet had sat prominently upon Old Mrs. Greeber's coffin. She, like many others at the funeral, had observed how lovely the white roses were with the ranunculus, ruscus, and salal tips... though it did seem odd that there was no baby's breath.

As the Queen would often say when irritated "She was not amused."

As the story goes, she bided her time for several months, into the summer, before she saw her chance for revenge. It was a Sunday afternoon, and at last she caught Zeb in a very vulnerable and hopefully uncomfortable position. He was under the car with only the bottom half of his torso exposed. For Fanny, this would be the coup de grace.

I can imagine her grin, even now.

She hurried on silent feet to the fridge and grabbed the jug of chilled water, cracking the tray of ice cubes into it for good measure.

Back out on the driveway, she tiptoed over to the car, bent, and yanked Zeb's zipper down. To her bemusement and irritation, he was wearing no underwear. She was religious about her laundry... that ungrateful man always had shorts to wear—stain-free too yet!

She heard Zeb gasp, but as he jerked in alarm, she poured the ice water, chortling gleefully.

"I got you! I got you! Let's freeze those bits, you're not using them for anything good anyhow!" And as the prostrate body squirmed and twisted, she shrieked in triumph. "I got you! I got you! I got you!"

And a few of the neighbours sidled out to watch. One of them had even managed to grab a beer on the way out.

Fanny's joy was giddy, unadulterated.

As she turned, still laughing hysterically, to run back into the house, a familiar figure strode out of the garage. "What're you on about?" The words came with a whiff of Old Man Greeber's hooch.

Fanny's blood must have been as frozen as her poor victim's nether-parts.

"Zeb? Where the hell? What? Who?" she stammered.

They both looked incredulously at the squirming, gasping, prostrate figure under their car. Then Zeb's face cracked into a smile so wide you could've slid a banana right in. "Is that any way to treat my brother Tom?" my uncle chastened as he pulled the trembling, traumatized Tom (whose zipper was still open) out from under the car. "He just came over to help fix the car, now see what you've done! Now aren't you ashamed of yourself?"

Chalk one up for Zeb.

UNCLE TOM'S DAWG

My Uncle Tom was what some people would dub a rugged individualist. Other observers, however, contended that he was stubborn and lazy and lacked common sense. Most of his relatives who knew him at all considered him a black sheep and a disgrace to the family's good name. He often leaped into the limelight, but seldom for positive reasons. Many were convinced that Tom was a profligate drunkard, a lazy layabout, and a perennial poacher. Even worse, he had been divorced twice. That was in the days before disespousal was universally accepted as normal. Tom wasn't home that much; he piloted an 18-wheeler semi-transport on long hauls to the States. It was a good job for him; he only had his weekends to get into trouble.

Tom's non-conformist attitude knew no bounds. He named his Heinz-57 variety dog, Dawg, an appellation cribbed from an American associate. He misspelled the name on Dawg's doghouse purposely, just to be cantankerous. Wherever Tom went, Dawg was never far behind. He reacted instinctively to Tom's slightest movements and mannerisms. Dawg was Tom's constant companion and best friend.

Dawg was not what you would call a cute canine. Even as a pup, he was homely and misshapen and drew both petulance and pity. Unkind observers called Dawg an ugly critter. But Tom loved him, and Dawg showed an infinite affection and unfailing loyalty for Tom. Tom and Dawg reveled in their raucous, devilish diversions.

Although Dawg's pedigree was uncertain, one thing was sure, Dawg was a mongrel. A tenuous cross between a bloodhound, an airedale, and a cocker spaniel, he retained the undesirable qualities and physical characteristics of each breed. His sad, droopy eyes were reminiscent of a basset hound. He had baggy lips that flapped like a horse's. His mottled gray and brown fur was mangy-looking even after his yearly bath in the marsh behind

Tom's house. The wrinkled skin on his forehead hung loosely over his eyes, giving him a pronounced Cro-Magnon look. Dawg even walked with a comical uneven gait, as if his left hip was locked, and he always seemed to be staggering sideways. Dawg barked with a weird rasp that resembled the guttural cough of a consumptive. Dawg was a weird, but wonderful creature.

Tom was incarcerated regularly in the local goal for various missteps (usually surrounding strong drink). Inevitably, Dawg would ensconce himself in the pound for some doggy misdeeds like crapping on the neighbour's lawn or spilling all the garbage cans on the street onto the road. Dawg was faithful that way.

Dawg's age was a mystery; they lost count at fourteen (98 in dog years). When Dawg bloated out too much and lost his trim figure, on advice from Tom's long-suffering wife Muriel, Tom got worried about his health (Dawg's, not Tom's) and came up with a diet and exercise program. He fed Dawg kibble for mature dogs, supplemented with canned horse meat, and quit feeding him scraps from the table. Dawg was not enamored with this new cuisine. Before long he went on a hunger strike and moped around with a woebegone look on his face. After a day or so Tom couldn't stand it anymore. He reverted to the old system where Dawg ate anything and everything. Dawg's gluttony was legend.

One night, Dawg gorged on a particularly large slab of greasy, fatty pork; he outdid himself. He bowed his head to the ground and choked. His windpipe was strangled by an obstruction of grease and fat that he could not dislodge despite his wheezing, coughing and howling. He released a terrible cacophony of yawps and yelps that were heard two blocks away. Fortunately, Tom was home; he quickly realized Dawg's peril and jumped into action, He grabbed him around the chest from behind a performed a doggy Heimlich maneuver. Dawg coughed a couple of times then gagged a hideous noise. A large gob of partially digested meat and stringy fat the texture of suet disgorged from Dawg's mouth and flew across the kitchen, flapping as it went. The unguided missile stuck high on the opposite wall with a thump—out of reach. It was still hanging there in the morning.

Diet control was unsuccessful, so Tom tried exercise. Tom's idea of a workout was to tie Dawg on a leash to his back bumper and drive slowly around the neighborhood with Dawg in toe. Dawg was not enamored with this procedure. He routinely hid either Tom's keys or the leash whenever he sensed Tom's fitness program approaching. Dawg was smart that way.

Dawg's nemesis was Cleo, a giant female calico cat that lived next door. Cleo was just as ornery as Dawg and relished in tormenting him. She gave him multiple scars on his nose from their regular altercations. Dawg got his own licks in though; he clamped her in his vice like jaws and shook her like a rag doll whenever he caught her. Neither had been seriously wounded, and over time they developed a reluctant respect for each other. They both seemed to love the competition for neighbourhood supremacy.

Cleo taunted Dawg by sitting on the edge of his property until he attacked with fang and claw. She then retreated by climbing up on the fence that divided the two yards and scampering back into the safety of her own space. This went on for an eternity, with Dawg always just about capturing the wily feline before she dashed up the fence and away. Finally, after numerous unsuccessful attempts, Dawg seemed to give up—so Cleo thought.

Dawg feigned apathy, never venturing off his porch, for a while until one Saturday afternoon in June when Tom was painting the fence that divided the two properties. Tom's first wife Lorraine had bugged him for months to do something about the ugly, peeling, eyesore. Tom's choice of color was a rusty red, not because it matched anything, but because there was a clearance special at Canadian Tire.

Dawg waited patiently until the fence was well lathered with the paint from the five-gallon pail. Cleo was perched in her regular spot, goading Dawg with flicks of her tail and shakes of her head. Dawg finally rushed her with great, galloping strides.

In her normal pattern, Cleo leaped up on the fence and started to rush to safety. She was immediately drenched on all four paws, legs, and her underbelly with the sticky, rust-red paint. She conceded defeat at the hands of a superior tactician by letting out a piercing caterwaul, her back hunched in dismay. Dawg was ecstatic; he ran parallel to her along the fence until she reached the end just in case she slipped on the slimy surface and fell off. He would like nothing better than to shake her one more time.

Cleo did not return to their open combat. She knew when she was beat. Her owner bathed her in varsol, and great patches of fur fell out until she looked like a plucked chicken. Cleo was too embarrassed to come around anymore. Dog didn't gloat much, that wasn't his style, but if a dog could grin, Dawg had a big, wide grin on his face.

After he defeated Cleo, Dawg took his job as resident watchdog more seriously. He staked out the territory around the yard as a no-go zone. Tom had developed an ingenious method of training Dawg to attack anyone who had the temerity to trespass on his property. He fashioned two scarecrows, one representing the mailman and the other the paperboy, dressed in authentic garb, and hung them on the clothesline. About once a week Tom could be seen moving the improvised targets back and forth on the clothesline with his dog chasing and biting them. Dawg became quite proficient in keeping any delivery people away. The mailman and paperboy refused to deliver to Tom's house. Delivery and service folk also gave Tom's house a wide berth. Lorraine was furious; tradesmen would not come to fix things around their dilapidated dwelling. Tom wasn't worried though. He said, "if the house falls apart, I'll burn it down."

Tom didn't mind much about the mailman and the paperboy; he couldn't read too good anyway and if he wanted something badly enough, he'd buy it in the States in his travels.

One day, Lorraine was taking her turn hosting the neighborhood coffee klatch. As the attending ladies arrived, Dawg was banished to the woodshed. Dawg did not take kindly to being evicted from his own territory. He formulated a plan to repel the invaders.

Dawg escaped the woodshed with ease (Tom just hadn't gotten around to fixing those loose boards in the back), ensconced himself in the bathroom, and waited for an unsuspecting intruder to arrive. When one finally came in, he immediately stuck his head in the toilet and started lapping and thrashing about spraying water all around. The trespasser took flight and warned the other infidels of the hideous monster in the loo.

Next, he went out to his house and gathered up the large malodorous, mummified rat he had been saving for just such an occasion and dropped it at Lorraine's feet. Then to complete the operation before the enemy could regain their balance, he did the rounds and licked the faces of all four of Lorraine's erstwhile guests. Dawg's plan worked like a charm. The coffee klatch scattered and did not return, nor was it likely to until Dawg was either dead or removed from the scene.

Neither Dawg nor Tom were very sociable. They were most disturbed when uninvited visitors showed up at their doorstep expecting to be fed and entertained. These pariahs were mostly from Lorraine's side of the family. Tom's relatives knew enough not to visit unless invited— and they were never invited. Tom's policy, shared by Dawg, was that relatives were like fish—after three hours they started to stink.

It was late on a Sunday afternoon, while Dawg and Tom were stretched out in the living room, snoring in symphony, when a tribe of Lorraine's relatives descended on the unsuspecting trio and ruined what had been until then a tranquil day. It was an hour before suppertime and Lorraine's brother and his wife and their brood of four kids dropped in for a few minutes on their way home to their farm in the next county. A few minutes stretched into a few hours and the guests reluctantly, feigning total embarrassment, not wanting to put anybody out, accepted the unsolicited, unexpected and unnecessary, invitation to dine.

The group showed up a second Sunday not long after, and then a third about a month later. Their freeloading was bad enough, but what galled Tom the most was, whenever the cleaning up started, it was the same pantomime each time.

"Let me help you with those dishes," the sister in law would insist, and grab a tea towel.

Then the brother would pipe up, "Sorry dear but we have to go. The chores are waiting remember?" Then they'd look sorrowfully at Lorraine and Tom and say, "You understand chores, right? A farmer's work is never done." And they would gather their well-stuffed brood and escape with what Tom considered undue haste.

On the third descent of the locusts, Tom and Dawg were ready. They devised an ingenious scheme to discourage the intrusions of the uninvited kinfolk. Everything was happening on schedule with the guests having eaten their fill and the hostess beginning to busy herself with the cleaning up.

"Let me help you with those dishes," came the customary offer from the sister-in-law. Just as the brother was about to offer regrets because of chores and all, Tom interjected.

"Oh, don't worry about the dishes, it's no problem now. We've come up with a new method for Sunday dishes since you people have been coming so regularly."

"Did you buy a dishwasher?"

Tom smirked at the brother. "Well, sort of, but not the plug-in type."

"How does it work?" The brother seemed puzzled.

"It's easy," Tom gestured toward Dawg who had just appeared in clear view of all the diners. He turned around three times, laid down and started lapping his not-unsubstantial crotch with gusto. "We put the dishes out by Dawg's house overnight and come morning they're clean as a whistle, ready to be stacked away for next Sunday dinner!"

The interlopers dashed out with a welcome undue haste and never showed up again.

Pity.

When Lorraine got a job at the laundromat, Dawg was left home alone with all means of escape locked or tightly sealed. He showed his displeasure by chewing up just about everything that belonged to Lorraine, including her underwear, (he didn't touch any of Tom's stuff). Tom solved the problem by quitting his job and going on the dole so that he could stay home with Dawg. Loyalty goes both ways, after all.

Dawg was omnivorous; he gobbled up just about anything, but his favorites were pizza and beer, which he gulped down in large quantities. This combination really gave him severe doggy breath and doggy gas. But Dawg had discriminating taste for his libations. He wouldn't drink just any beer. He had his own brand; Molson's Ex—and he knew the difference. This strange talent of Dawg's proved to be Uncle Tom's undoing.

Tom was a veteran beer drinker in his own right. And since his wife wouldn't go drinking at the local tavern with him, he took Dawg along for company. Tom won many free beers displaying Dawg's perceptive palate. As a bonus, he discovered that Dawg could always find the way home. This was especially handy on the occasions when Tom drank one or two (or three) too many. After a while this started to happen regularly and nobody, it appeared, was ever the worse off, except maybe Lorraine.

As luck would have it, disaster struck one night when Tom, as usual, had that one too many and Dawg was charged again with navigating home. The problem was that, that night, old Dawg had drunk almost as much beer as Tom. In the wee hours of the morning, Dawg deposited a drunken, bilious Tom, safe and sound, into the house. Then Tom puked his guts out; after watching Tom, Dawg puked his innards up also. Neither Dawg nor Tom, it appears, were house broken. They stuck together in fair times and foul.

This was foul.

Unfortunately, Dawg in his befuddled state lead the pair to the wrong house. It was the house next door—where some in-laws lived. They were most displeased, to say the least, with this late-night visit from their raunchy relatives. There's that old joke about the difference between in-laws and outlaws—outlaws are wanted.

Dawg and Tom alienated mother-in-law, father-in-law, and wife in one fell sweep. It's an understatement that they were both in the doghouse. Not long after, Lorraine (on advice from her mother) had had enough of Tom and Dawg's antics and left the pair to their own devices. It was a sad day. Tom tried to feign remorse, but Dawg was ecstatic.

After two days of mourning, Dawg and Tom decided it was time to go courting— together. Dawg had taken an interest in the Widow Ellie Strachan's poodle, Poopsie. As for Tom, he coveted the widow's 4x4 Chevy Silverado left by her dearly departed husband.

Dawg was lovesick. He howled and wailed and bayed at the moon and made the most awful commotion until Tom was coerced into making some excuse to visit the widow and Poopsie. Around Poopsie, Dawg got quite romantic. Whenever he saw her, he went into an animated love dance. He crouched low, extended his forepaws out straight, and cocked his head to the side. If she came near he threw his forelegs around her neck and wrestled her to the ground. This was followed by much chasing and running—Dawg chasing and Poopsie running. Dawg's efforts continued for a couple of months until finally the widow took a shine to Tom. This was teamwork at its best.

Not long after, Dawg and Poopsie and Tom and Ellie were wed in a simple double ceremony with minimum attendance in the widow's back yard. Everything was going along great. Tom had the 4x4; the widow wasn't a widow anymore; Dawg had Poopsie; and Poopsie had Dawg. Win, win, win, and win.

But connubial bliss was not to last.

To start with, Dawg and Poopsie had a falling out. Dawg had a peculiar habit. He scrubbed his rump on the ground routinely, in the dirt in the front yard, shortly after breakfast, every morning. This ritual took place when most of the neighbors passed by on their way to work. Dawg extended his back legs up over his head and shunted along ground on his butt, dragging himself forward with his front paws. He relished the attention this received; but Poopsie, it seems, took offence. One morning after Dawg had put on a particularly disgusting display, she ran away and was never seen or heard of again.

Dawg was heart-broken. To relieve his suffering, Tom let him sleep inside the house instead of in the lonely double-dog kennel the widow had constructed for him and his bride. It started innocently enough, Dawg slept in the corner of the kitchen by the wood stove. But before long he was in the hallway, and then he advanced to the foot of their bed, and one night Dawg jumped in and cuddled up right in between Tom and the widow like the camel that sticks it's nose under the tent flap and before long he owns the tent.

"I'll not put up with that smelly dog in bed with us," Ellie insisted.

"Aw, he's alright," Tom said. "He's just lonely since Poopsie ran off."

The former widow—who had already begun to wonder if it wouldn't have been wiser for her to stay that way—wasn't having it. "But, what about the stench?"

Tom shrugged. "Don't worry about it. Old Dawg don't mind a little stink. He's used to it."

The next day a sign appeared on the dog kennel in front of the widow's house: "FOR SALE—NEW DOG HOUSE. SUITABLE FOR TWO DOGS OR ONE HUSBAND."

Scratch Wife Number Two.

Tom's sorrow there was that he didn't get to keep the 4X4.

Dawg and Tom soon settled back into their pedestrian pursuits. Hunting was one of these. Both Dawg and Tom were sometimes struck with an irresistible primordial urge for the chase. Dawg wasn't interested in chasing anything that was too fast, like rabbits (running wasn't one of Dawg's strong suits), and besides, old Tom wasn't a very good shot and his eyesight was starting to fail. Anything moving, even crawling—forget it (not to mention Dawg's own safety). When deer hunting, season arrived, Dawg and Tom finally got to display their hunting skills.

It was a crisp autumn evening, and Dawg and Tom were out on one of their nocturnal drives in the country in his dilapidated '89 Ford pickup called old Saul, (remember; the widow took the

4X4 back). Old Saul was one big ball of smoke and rust. He chugged and moaned his way down the road with parts flopping off every quarter. Saul was shod with bald tires with cords hanging out of them. He announced his coming about two minutes before arrival with rattling and squealing and the habitual billowing black smoke screen. Old Saul was long overdue for the wrecking yard. Tom had to take the back roads so the cops wouldn't stop him and take him off the road and cite him for driving a dangerous vehicle. He always intended to get a better truck, (fit for the road) but the monthly beer and pizza bill, for him and Dawg, always ate up any spare funds.

So they were driving that night. Dawg was in his usual position, in the passenger's seat, paws on the dashboard, peering imperiously out the window to make sure he didn't miss anything. It was along about twilight when Dawg spied a couple of deer watering at a stream about fifty yards off the road. He yelped and yapped frantically and leaped around inside the cab like a mad person until Tom had to stop. The two deer, a handsome buck and a large doe, remained in position—motionless.

Goaded on by Dawg's ballyhoo barking, and agitated pointing, Tom reached for his shotgun and pumped about five slugs into the stag and another half dozen into the doe, reloading three times. They still didn't go down. Either those were the toughest deer in history, Tom's aim was getting far worse, or there was something else amiss.

Indeed, it was Option Number Three.

A platoon of game wardens immediately descended on the two poachers with spot lights and loud hailers. A couple of stuffed deer, strategically positioned to ensnare the likes of Dawg and Tom, had worked to a tee.

It was jail and pound for Tom and Dawg.

Again.

After the report of this incident filtered through the family grapevine, a blinding flash of the obvious finally struck us. All of Tom's problems, all his adventures and intrigues, had one common denominator.

Dawg.

Dawg was leading Tom astray. Dawg was the brains of the outfit. It was all Dawg's fault, the arrests, the divorces, the drunken escapades, even the unemployment, was all due not to Tom, but to his canine companion.

Speculation among the more enlightened kinsfolk was that Dawg was empowered with a mysterious intelligence, which he used mystically to control Tom's mind. This was why Tom had no self-discipline and could never behave himself. It was obvious. Tom was just a scapegoat. It wasn't Uncle Tom's Dawg after all; it was Dawg's Uncle Tom. It seemed that Tom was under a psychic canine spell; Dawg was the planner, the coordinator and the executor of their many mischievous and malevolent behaviour. Dawg chased away both of Tom's wives and refused to allow him to marry again.

Now, whenever I visit back home, Dawg/Tom's house is in total disrepair, because Dawg won't let anybody, friend or foe, on his property. But, Tom's relatives were relieved, at least, to finally realize that it was Dawg, not Tom initiating all the shenanigans that they got into.

When I see Dawg, Uncle Tom is never far behind. And when the scuttlebutt gets around about their latest misadventures, I wonder.

It might be my imagination, but when I see Dawg looking at Tom, I swear he's looking at him with the proprietary grin of a father for a favored son. And whenever I hint at these suspicions to Uncle Tom, he just gazes affectionately at Dawg with a servile smile..

"Everything is going to the dogs" I joked to Tom one day—but I don't think he got my point.

But when I looked at Dawg, I saw a slow deliberate wink from his lazy left eye—Dawg got it.

They say what goes around comes around.

Hear, Hear

My late grandmother, Catherine (Nanny to the family), was an inspiring matriarch to scores of offspring who stretched over four generations. Widowed young, she raised her family by herself. Even after she bore seven children, grandmothered twenty-two, great-grandmothered fourteen and great-great-grandmothered three, she was still a force to be reckoned with.

Over the years, Nanny developed a great deal of self-reliance and independence. She did all the things a grandmother should do and more. Her memory was phenomenal; she knew all her kin's names, birthdays, eye and hair colouring, and even how they were progressing at school. She offered her sage, grandmotherly advice on child-rearing techniques and home remedies freely, whether anyone requested them or not. You could cure earaches by blowing tobacco smoke into the offending ear; a spoon of brown sugar with a couple of drops of turpentine prevented worms. Nanny was a fount of knowledge; even the neighbors called her Nanny and sought her advice.

Nanny's steadfast strength of character and dauntless perseverance came from her Irish heritage. She was descendant of the Irish immigrants that settled in northeastern New Brunswick in the 1850's after the Irish famine. Her single-minded resolution was of the old school. She was a loyal and devoted friend, but she could also be a fearsome, unyielding, and ruthless enemy.

She took in boarders for extra money after her husband died and her children left home. One border kept coming in late and drunk, well after Nanny's bedtime. After several warnings, she locked all the doors and threw the man's belongings out on the front step, in the snow. Noting this, the rest of her roomers were careful not to rile Nanny, especially in the winter. Pour les autres?

"If you're in Nanny's good books you're OK, but don't cross her or you're in trouble" her second oldest son Bobby, (Junior, to the family) commented one day with a determined look on his face. His steely expression could only be genealogically rooted, and we all knew precisely from where those roots sprung.

Nanny had an unlimited store of energy and stamina. Her persistence, once she made up her mind, was legend. Some of her family called her stubborn; others called her determined and still others called her obstinate; but nobody called her delicate or capricious. And Nanny was not about to change.

At the ripe-old age of 92, she was still a prolific shopper, maintained a flair for fashion and never appeared in public without her makeup. (She started dying her hair red at 60 and it was still red in her casket at 96). Nanny was indefatigable, and she reveled in the attention of her many relations, acquaintances, and friends who came to see her—if they could find her home.

Her infirmities were few for a nonagenarian. Although she suffered slightly from arthritis, she had acute vision, her mind was active and alert, and she walked consistently on her regular rounds of visits to her relatives and infinite in-laws. Her hearing loss, however, was a continuing nuisance. Hearing aids and sound-enhancing devices were naught but an annoyance to Nanny. But if the truth were known, she simply couldn't countenance anybody thinking she was a senior citizen. Nanny could pass for 60 when she was 80. She'd often say that "growing old is not for weaklings, you have to fight it every step of the way." And she did.

On the surface, at least she accepted her disability, with cheerful resolution, as permanent and non-correctable. There was nothing she could do about it. And, if the truth be known; sometimes it could work to her advantage.

"Nanny's as deaf as a post," her eldest granddaughter Maggee would often say.

"You have to yell and stare Mom in the face or she'll never understand you," the middle of her three sons, Jason, insisted. "I think she can read lips" he added.

After a while everybody in the extended family accepted their senior living ancestor's infirmity as a minor inconvenience. As far as they were concerned, she was deaf and that was it; they'd have to work around it.

I'm not exactly sure when, but I started to have my doubts about the extent of Nanny's hearing impairment as time went on. I was not really convinced that she was as deaf as everyone believed. She didn't hear the telephone—or knocks on the door—if it was someone that she was not interested in talking to, but she heard noises two blocks away if one of her many grandchildren were involved. I began to believe she actually suffered from could be called selective hearing loss. "She heard what she wanted to hear," her daughter Daisy recounted, "and she blotted the rest out." And she guarded her secret well.

It was to take a door-to-door fund raising canvasser from an obscure historical society in the Miramichi valley to put grandmother's hearing capabilities under serious scrutiny.

It was late June, and the sweet fragrance of her lilac bushes was in the air. She was alone at home when a warming afternoon sun was high in the sky. A stout middle-aged man in a gray and brown seer-sucker suit showed up on her doorstep. In his left hand, he carried a dark brown briefcase like the ones that the insurance salesmen have. The man pounded prodigiously at the door until Nanny finally answered.

The smiling seer-sucker suit became animated and immediately spieled out his prepared speech with breathless energy and too many smiles for Nanny's liking.

"Good afternoon Madam," the man said, full of flattery and taking off his fedora style hat with a flourish. "Is the lady of the house, at home?" he said, "You're far too young to be....

"Eh?" grandmother interrupted, with a puzzled expression, cupping her hand over her ear.

He repeated his salutation, a good deal louder, and more pronounced, and got the same response. Recognizing his task, the canvasser launched into the rest of his sales speech in a higher pitch. "I'm collecting for the Upper Miramichi Valley Historical Society," he yelled. "We're trying to preserve the heritage of our ancestors."

"Eh?" Nanny repeated once more, a little louder.

"I'm collecting for the Upper Miramichi Valley Historical Society!" he hollered, forty decibels higher, pronouncing each word separately with conviction. "We're trying...

"Eh!" Nanny interrupted, louder still.

Finally, admitting defeat, the fund-raising representative from the Upper Miramichi Valley Historical Society, turned on his heels and unceremoniously departed, his shoes scraping deliberately on the scaly, peeling steps.

"Mind you close that gate, young feller," grandmother shouted after him with a serious tone.

"To hell with your gate!" the canvasser said, to himself, in the sibilance of a whisper, as he closed the rickety gate, a little harder than he had to, and strode stiffly down the street, his briefcase swinging higher than normal.

With a glint of mischief in her eye and an unmistakable look of triumph Nanny gave her reply—loudly and distinctly.

"And to hell with you and your Upper Miramichi Valley Historical Society too!"

Uncle Jake

My Uncle Jake was what could only be labeled as a pampered husband. Jake was an only child, born years after his parents had given up on ever having offspring, and even his mother, Margaret, who was partially responsible for his condition, freely admitted that he was spoiled rotten. He acted like a guest in his own home. Jake had what in modern parlance is called a severe sense of entitlement. So grateful to have a child of her own, his mother fussed over him like he was a newborn; she, did everything for him. She cleaned up after him, and washed and ironed his clothes, even when he became a messy, moody, ungrateful teenager.

Jake's sloth knew no bounds. He would sleep late most mornings and had to be roused several times before he got up to go to school. On weekends, he seldom got out of bed before noon. His chores around the house included taking the garbage out once a week and cutting their lawn, which was a about half the size of a badminton court. Even these minor tasks were constantly neglected and ignored. Jake would only move, after much coaxing, when the lawn became a hayfield and clouds of fruit flies buzzed around the discarded fruit and vegetable leavings and squirrels and racoons took up residence around the garbage pails.

After high school, he got a job taking tickets at the local movie theatre. He sat on a stool and took people's money and handed them their movie ticket. He stayed at that job his whole working life.

His mother continued to do his laundry, ironing and even made his bed long after the time that most young men were doing their own. Jake stayed at home until he was almost thirty. That was when he married Annette Twindles, who was pushing thirty herself and desperate to end her status as 'spinster.' Though she was a kind, sweet woman, Annette's rather long, horse-ish face and shy demeanour had made it difficult to land herself a husband. Margaret had orchestrated the whole thing, deciding that Annette would be grateful enough to be married that she'd put up even with Jake.

He was just as helpless as a husband as he was as a son, probably more so. Soon after Jake's marriage, Margaret went on to her eternal rest—a rest she likely needed quite badly. Margaret left behind a not-insignificant amount of money... blessedly, under the authority of her brother George. When Jake made noises about quitting his job, George set the money in trust to give Jake a monthly income that, when combined with his modest earnings from the movie theatre, would give the newlyweds a comfortable, but not extravagant life. If Jake quit his job or reduced his hours, George would turn off the taps. That threat was the only thing that kept Jake at his job.

Annette followed her long-suffering mother-in-law's habit; she did everything for him. She cooked all his favourite dishes, she went to all the sporting events that Jake liked (she hated sports), and rumour has it that she even ironed Jake's underwear and socks—if you can imagine that. But that's how Margaret had done it, and that's how Jake liked it. Annette, being a newlywed who had been rather fond of her mother-in-law in the brief time she'd known her, was determined to honour the poor soul in any way she could.

The rest of the family was not so charitable. His cousin Jim would often say that "Jake has a chronic disease—laziness—and a severe allergy to any form of work."

Uncle George fully agreed and added his own assessment that "Jake is as lazy as a fat cat; he could make an idle fat cat look lively and energetic." He wouldn't even put his dirty clothes in the hamper and regularly threw them on the floor in a trail across the bedroom floor. When the pile got too high, he hid them under the bed (and Annette dutifully searched the garments out and picked up). As a rule, he would put on the cleanest—read least dirty—clothes on after a cursory inspection by sniffing them.

Jake didn't know how the clothes washer worked, he had no idea how to operate the dryer, and he couldn't turn the dishwasher on if his life depended on it. He tried once, but somehow ended up spurting water all over the floor. Not long after, he put way too much soap in the washer and ended up with couple of feet of foam spilling from the laundry room right out to the front door.

After that, he never tried again, and Annette never asked him to.

The popular consensus was that without Annette, he would have quickly starved to death or died of some horrible infectious disease from complete lack of hygiene.

His complete and all-encompassing dependence on his wife was clearly illustrated when my aunt went into the hospital for their first child. Jake was to be left to his own devices for three whole days. Annette expected a disaster if Jake did not have adult supervision (her words). She had nightmares of the house burning down or being flooded out. After much coaxing and cajoling from Annette, her mother Joyce reluctantly 'volunteered' to come and do the house-keeping and look after Jake while Annette was giving birth.

For the first couple of days everything seemed to be going well with mother-in-law and son-in-law peacefully co-existing. On detailed instructions from her daughter, mother-in-law did her best to cater to Jake's every whim (managing somehow to keep her temper and remain somewhat civil).

However, this armistice was not to last.

It had been almost a day and a half since mother-in-law Joyce arrived and the pressure was starting to build and show some cracks in the seams of Joyce's patience. Jake's incessant demands were starting to wear her down, and she began to get a little testy. The crisis came when she finally got to sit down and rest after a long arduous day of cooking and cleaning and running about the house looking after her totally incapable charge.

"Would you mind, Joy," (Jake called his mother-in-law Joy—she hated that—he knew that, but persisted) "getting me a glass of water?"

"I just got you one, not ten minutes ago, Jake," Joyce said with a faint indulgent smile. "I'm really tired, could you possibly get your own water this time, just for once?"

Much to his mother-in-law's surprise Jake agreed.

"Sure, no problem, Joy," he said, (she grimaced) as he got up from his permanent, glued on position, on the lazy-boy. A few minutes later, however, Jake came back with a quizzical look on his face, and asked sheepishly, "Ah, ah Joy, just one question; where do we keep our glasses?"

With all the control she could muster, Joyce managed to answer him politely. "They're in the right-hand cupboard above the microwave" she said, smiling again, through clenched teeth.

"Thanks," said Jake, grinning absently. But a few seconds later, he returned waving an empty glass.

"Ah, ah, Joy one more question, if I may."

"What is it now?" Joyce snapped. Her poor daughter would be coming home to take care of two infants, it would seem.

In his most helpless, pitiful, pose Jake asked, "Where do we keep our water?"

Uncle Perce

Back in the fifties, my great uncle Perce was an early version of what is now ostentatiously called a meteorological technician or less loftily, perhaps, a weather man. Perce was a fair to middling farmer, but what he became renown for in our hometown area was his uncanny and sagely accurate weather predictions. He foresaw thunderstorms, squalls, and even unseasonal sunshine and unwarranted winds. Perce's left eye was glass, which made him look even more mystifying. Many of his neighbour's referred to him as Merlin the Magician or even an older, less-handsome, Houdini. Perce liked the Houdini similarity comparison better.

The consensus, in the county, was that old Perce possessed, an ethereal, supernatural power that allowed him to foretell fluctuations and changes in normal weather patterns. Uncle Perce was constantly questioned on how he could tell whether the next day's atmospheric prospects would be foul or fair. He always just smiled and insisted that it was a secret told to him by an old Indigenous medicine man he once knew. If he betrayed the medicine man's trust, he would say, his divining skills would be lost forever, in the mists of time. (Perce like to talk about 'the mists of time' for some reason).

Friends and relatives attempted for years to coax his magic from him, but Perce remained stalwart. His answer was always the same, drunk or sober, day or night. It seemed that the secret would die with old Perce and there was no sense in trying to get him to betray the medicine man's trust. Perce was loyal and faithful if nothing else.

But two of my uncles, Tom and George, as a personal challenge, decided to try to wrestle their uncle Perce's surreptitious secret from him. They schemed for months trying to come up with some Machiavellian method to rest Perce's secret from him. They even started watching uncle Perce's every move for hints and clues to the source of his mysterious powers. Tom would ask him a battery of carefully worded leading questions designed to trap him. George would then repeat the same queries in a different sequence, with varied words and phrases. Next, the two interrogators would compare notes to see if Perce had revealed anything incriminating. Tom even hid up in a tree bordering Perce's property to observe every move he made for 24 hours. George hid in the loft of his barn, again, for over 24 hours to stand sentry to discover if Perce had any magic in the barn or attached to his animals. This was a rabid hunt.

The inquisitors would show up at all hours of the day or night in an attempt to catch the sorcerer with his secret potions. Poor Perce was under constant, unrelenting siege. They gave him no rest. Perce was, to say the least, getting fed up. He developed a scheme of his own to put the hounds off his trail.

Finally, it appeared that Perce was starting to weaken. He could not, it seemed, endure the badgering any longer. He told Tom and George that if they would swear and hope to die, if they ever told a soul, he would tell them his secret. He told them, confidentially, that he was subjecting himself to torture and certain death or dismemberment if the medicine man ever learned that he had betrayed his trust. So, they must take a blood oath not to reveal it. Tom and George weren't sure what a blood oath was, but they were willing to give it a try.

They eagerly agreed, and very reluctantly, Perce consented to show them how he was able to predict the weather. But, he would only show them in his barn, after midnight, and under the light of his old kerosene hurricane lamp. These were Perce's conditions. Again, the nephews excitedly nodded their approval. They would do just about anything to uncover the secret. He had them in his grip.

The night of revelation was a blustery, cool spring evening with no moon. It was pitch black in the barn with only the flicker of the kerosene lamp to give a faint fleeting light to Uncle Perce's demonstration. Tom and George were seated, awe struck, in a trance, on hay bales giving their full attention to Perce's every move and utterance. Perce was in full control.

Perce was standing erect, in front of his nephews with what appeared to be a length of one-inch hemp rope in his left hand. The rope was about thirty inches long with one end frayed and the other end tightly bound with electrical tape. There was a white marking at about mid-level.

"This is my secret," Perce declared, his dark eyes blazing, even in the half light - his glass eye glinting with a reptilian stare.

"But, but, how does it work?" Tom and George chorused, unable to contain their enthusiasm. Perce had their undivided attention, "for the first time," he later said.

"Well" said Perce, "It's like this you see. When I want to know what the weather's going to be like the next day, I hang the frayed end of this rope out my bedroom window, when I go to bed at night, at the half measure of the rope. Remember it has to be exactly at the half way white mark—fifteen inches precisely—not a quarter inch less or a quarter inch more," he emphasized in his deep baritone. Perce continued with a diabolical look on his countenance. "Then I close the window tight, on the rope, before I go to sleep."

"Yes, but how do you tell whether it's going to be windy, or rain or shine?" the nephews questioned in unison, jumping up off their seats, almost stumbling over each other. Perce was enjoying this.

"Now that's simple," Perce continued, grinning broadly, with a mischievous glint in his dark eye and with his glass eye shining brightly from the reflection of the lamp. "In the morning, if the rope's flopping up and down it'll be windy! If the rope's wet, we're in for rain! But if the rope's dry, we'll have sunshine!"

The nephews both fell off their perch on the hay bales. The magician had tricked them, and now it was their secret that they wanted guarded. Uncle Perce solemnly promised he would tell no one, especially the family, but unfortunately (for Tom and George) it got out somehow, even though Perce had sworn silence and hoped to die, if he ever told a soul of Tom and George's secret. George and Tom were the laughingstock of the family, and the town, and even the county for a long time.

When asked Perce said, with his trademark grin, that "the cows must have told."

My great uncle Perce unfortunately is long since gone on to his eternal reward. We now should rely on the vagaries of modern technology for our daily weather reports.

BIG TURKEY

My Uncle Clarence and Aunt Myrtle were an ornery pair. They seldom exchanged more than a couple of comparatively civil sentences a week. Each of them seemed to take a devilish, diabolical, pleasure in constantly cursing, insulting and berating the other. Their constant state of conflict was legend. They were not unlike the Hatfields and the McCoys, but without guns—we think. Both of them died of natural causes, so we're fairly comfortable in that estimation.

Folks in town often said that Uncle Clarence was a slightly taller and equally bald "Don Rickles—only nastier." (And he didn't put it on). With her trademark sarcasm, whenever she had an audience of one or more, Myrtle would relate that Clarence "had a wide part." Aunt Myrtle could make Phyllis Diller blush, the neighbours often said. Clarence relished pointing out that she had the same hair style as Ms. Diller.

Their incessant bickering became legend in the family.

Aunt Myrtle reveled in revealing an embarrassing story about Uncle Clarence whenever she could until it was cemented in family lore. Uncle Clarence was a truck driver and he plowed the 401 Highway between Trenton and Belleville in the winter. After several years of this sitting on cold seats, at subzero temperatures, for twelve-hour shifts, he developed a bad case of piles, hemorrhoids to the more delicate amongst us.

Myrtle tended to tell the story with devilish delight. One cold, blustery, January night, Clarence returned from ploughing all night to the warmth of his house, if not the warmth of his wife. Aunt Myrtle heard him groan as he got into bed (this made her happy). She pretended to be asleep so he wouldn't have to tell her about his long, arduous and painful night on the road. She was thoughtful that way.

About an hour later Clarence got up and rummaged around the night stand, looking for his jar of Vaseline to apply to his tender, itching piles. "Unfortunately,", Aunt Myrtle repeated (often) in a gleeful, sarcastic, tone "Clarence grabbed my jar of vapo-rub instead of his Vaseline." At this point, she would bray like a donkey before she composed herself enough to continue with the tale. She was in her glory telling this one if she had the rapt attention of relatives or friends who hadn't heard the tale before. Family gatherings would always bring this one up again, and the new crop of in-laws and outlaws (as well as those polite enough to pretend they hadn't heard it) provided an audience.

Clarence usually stood at a distance, totally ignoring his wife and getting drunk with his brother Harold.

"Well," Myrtle would, with a giant grin on her face, eyes lit with excitement, "I heard this scream; I thought Clarence had seen a ghost or had a heart attack or something. But, when I turned the light on, he was scrubbing his rump around on the rug like a dog." She would then proceed to demonstrate how a dog would scrub its butt on the floor.

At this point Myrtle inevitably started to bray like a donkey again, only this time with a symphony of snorts and grunts. The assembled audience would laugh. It got to the point where Clarence wasn't even embarrassed any more. He just stood stoically in the corner with a look of impending revenge on his face.

Yeah, she even told that tale at his funeral. He probably knew it would happen, and he had probably looked forward to the fact that he wouldn't be able to hear it. Blessed eternal rest and all.

Now, don't go feeling too sorry for him. Clarence had his own tales for whenever he could gather listeners together. Which was often. Though I'm certain he considered himself fortunate to die before her, I'm sure he regretted that he was unable to tell the following story on her.

Myrtle was hosting a twelfth birthday party for their eldest daughter Emily. She had invited about two dozen of Emily's raucous friends and relatives; the scene was pandemonium.

They played a quick game of pin the tail on the donkey, but it was short-lived because on kid stuck the pin fully into another kid's arm, obviously due to what Clarence called "a serious lack of supervision" on Myrtle's part.

After the hubbub with the pin sticking incident settled down, with no better options, Myrtle decided that it was time to eat. She left the kids to one of the volunteer mothers to hand out paper plates and plastic utensils, serve the vegetable and fruit trays and crackers and cheese, while she put the finishing touches on the chocolate cake. When she got to the final icing of the giant dessert, she realized that she hadn't put the cubes of dark chocolate in the mix. She quickly reached for the box on the top shelve of the cupboard, out of reach of her ravenous offspring, and threw it into the reheated icing sugar, bubbling in a large pot on the stove. All was going well, so the hostess thought.

Myrtle didn't find out until a couple of days later that she had caused an outbreak of communal, contagious diarrhea. She had mistakenly cooked a large cube of laxative into the birthday cake mixings. Just about all the mothers called her to complain. All the party-goers had had a bad experience about a day after the party, some more serious than others.

"My Georgie crapped his pants at school," one irate mother related, "he was so embarrassed!"

"No wonder" Clarence quipped, "that little hog had three pieces of cake; it's a wonder he made it home."

"My Sheila was at ballet when it happened; what a mess!" another mother lamented. "And now she's been demoted from Marie to a sugar plum fairy!"

After hearing several similar stories of 'Populous excreta' Myrtle was crestfallen (briefly), but Clarence was delighted. He now had a story to rival the vapo-rub rube. Whenever Myrtle made a cake, chocolate or otherwise, Clarence could not help but bring up the subject.

"Cousin Chester looks like he needs and enema; could you send him a piece of your cake." was his favorite."

Perhaps the biggest turkey of them all happened one Yuletide season, when Myrtle had volunteered to have the extended family multitude over for a formal turkey dinner on the Sunday before Christmas. Aunt Janet and Uncle Clem would come with their brood of eight kids. The eldest, cousins Mary and Jim, would eat a couple of pounds of turkey each. And the youngest, Harry and Kate, would eat a dozen desserts each. However, expecting this, Janet always brought more than her share of entrees, pop, and desserts for their growing, gluttonous kids.

After taking sums, Myrtle calculated that, including infants and infirm, the throng would number almost fifty. Uncle Tom and his latest wife (nobody could remember her name) would get drunk shortly after they arrived and start a big fight, with either other relatives or between themselves. Brother George and sister-in-law Ethel would turn their nose up at just about everything and talk about all their new possessions procured since the Christmas before (the family could only stand them once a year).

Sister Margaret would soon get into her cups and tell everybody who she didn't like, which was well, everybody, in her inimitable way, that "they would shit if they were well fed." She was quite a philosopher. She didn't discriminate.

The family always waited for this and goaded Margaret on because they knew that the insufferable George and wife Ethel would run off in a huff. Cousins Charlie and Alvin would always get into a fistfight over some past dispute, rumoured to be a marijuana sale gone amiss.

Despite, all this Myrtle started to put an operational plan together. The list of required victuals was enormous. About twenty-five pounds of potatoes and ten pounds each of carrots, turnips, and peas made up the vegetables. The gravy and dressing were prepared in two large eight-quart pots. The desserts, including Christmas fruit cake, cheesecake, and pies (mincemeat, apple, and pumpkin) were lined up, covering a ten-foot side table. The libations included a moose milk punch, plenty of beer and wine, and just about every brand of liquor, and a nonalcoholic pink lemonade for the kids under fourteen.

At the top of the list was a turkey weighing in at a minimum of forty pounds. Being stubborn, like she tended to be, Myrtle was determined not to send anyone home without stuffing them so full of cornbread dressing they rivalled the turkey. The last time she'd hosted a holiday feast, cousin Jake threw up out the back door on the dog. The dog was not happy. He'd rolled around in the snow for about half an hour with a definite look of disgust on his face and barked whenever he saw cousin Jake for several years later, especially when Christmas came around. Myrtle insisted indignantly that it was the strong drink, not her food, that made Jake sick.

So… a few days before the event, Clarence had an opinion. "Won't fit," was what he said.

Myrtle, of course, had to snap back at him. "What won't fit?"

"Yer turkey," my uncle returned. I imagine that he had an unmistakably devious grin on his face. I believe it must have been the expression of Jack Nicholson's Joker in the Batman movie. I imagine he was also thinking about *One Flew Over the Cuckoo's Nest*, and how this party would be reminiscent of the actions of the mental patients in that award-winning show.

I know the conversation because they related it to me… but all I needed were the words. Their expressions and tones were easy to guess. Here would be where Myrtle started howling. "If the turkey won't fit, why didn't you tell me before now?"

Clarence apparently gave her a look of concern and commiseration, but I'm sure he was rather elated. He didn't hide it well for more than a few moments… he was snickering under his breath. And Myrtle was not amused. She was never amused. Cousin Bradley once said that he thought "he saw Myrtle smile once; but she must have had gas."

Clarence was rather spiteful in his response. He thought she knew. He thought she could see it was too big… any moron could see that the oven was too big for a forty-pound turkey. He was now bent over with belly laughs and could hardly walk—or talk (which didn't bother Myrtle).

"Get your coat on Clarence, we're going to buy a new stove right now," my aunt blurted. She would not be deterred, either by Clarence or a team of horses, and soon they found themselves rushing downtown with undue haste in their antique old Pontiac station wagon, with Myrtle critiquing Clarence's every move in the car and guiding him breathlessly to the Bay, which was the closest retailer with large appliances.

Inside the store, Myrtle stampeded about like a raging bull in search of the stove. Clarence was close behind, trying desperately not to snicker, (with limited success), but again pretending to be supportive whenever his wife looked at him, which was often. He was enjoying every minute of his latest effort at tormenting her.

But she was not to be outdone.

"I need a range with a very large oven," she blurted impatiently to the balding clerk with a terrible comb-over. "It has to hold at least a forty-pound turkey."

"Why this one here should do," the salesman pointed proudly to the largest stove on the floor, a black and stainless-steel monster which appeared to have way too many buttons and dials and red warning lights and alarms. "I guarantee that it has ample room for the biggest turkey you'll ever find in this town."

Aunt Myrtle considered his challenge. She looked at the stove, then she looked at the balding salesman with the terrible comb-over and pin-neat suit, then she looked at bald Uncle Clarence with his wide part, and then she looked at the stove again. She even went over and caressed the flat top of the stainless-steel monster like one would pet a favourite dog.

"This is really the biggest range that you have in the store? You're sure it will hold a forty-pound turkey?"

"Yes, I'm sure of it; we go on courses, you know, to learn these things," the salesman said with a hint of indignation.

"Yeah, turkey school" Uncle Clarence blurted out, then doubled over, again, with laughter.

Blushing somewhat, either from frustration or annoyance, the salesman repeated, "Believe me lady, I've never seen a turkey too big to fit into this model; you've probably got enough room to put your veggies and dressing in at the same time."

"Biggest turkey in town?" Myrtle asked one more time.

"I promise, lady. Probably the biggest turkey in the province."

That was just the set-up she needed. Though I was not there, and she's been gone a long time, I can still see clear as day the way her eyes would have sparkled as she ordered, "get in, Clarence... let's see if this thing will hold you!"

She never said it straight out, but I know that must have been the best moment of Myrtle's life. Especially after that poor salesclerk fell over from laughing so hard.

PART 2

EVERYDAY PEOPLE

THE THONG SHOW

It was Friday morning in early April, and winter was still about. Alice Christie rummaged methodically through a shipment of vacation clothes and separated them carefully by size, colour and cost. Everything would have its own place.

"The presentation has to be perfect," she muttered to herself, "or it's not worth doing. We give the best customer experience in town." She'd long been mocked for her habit of talking to herself, but she found that it helped keep her organized, and that was too important to her.

Her setup was not unlike the Dewey decimal system used by libraries. It was hardly less complicated.

It was almost noon, but Cayman Clothiers, her avant-garde swim and cabana wear shop in Kingston, was void of customers. The last snowbirds had yet to return from their winter nests in Florida, and locals were just coming out of hibernation.

Alice and her partner, Bonnie Johnson, a classmate from the fashion marketing course at St Lawrence College, feverishly prepared displays for the summer season. Both owners had sunk their life savings into the shop. Their business plan was sound, but unseasonably cold weather for the first two years had threatened liquidation, even bankruptcy. Marketing schemes of giveaway merchandise and trips to the Caribbean had barely broken even.

"God, I hope we make a profit this year, "Alice mumbled to no one; "I can't keep going back to Brian," (her MBA husband, nickname Elevator, was quickly going to the top) "to bail me out." She desperately needed to see some black on the ledger. The financial troubles had been causing tension between her and Bonnie, each blaming the other for marketing failures and low sales. Bonnie had been particularly critical of Alice's promotional ideas, insisting that she was hopelessly old-fashioned about it all.

The jangle of the phone interrupted her thoughts. "Cayman Clothiers," Alice sang sweetly with a hint of Maritime lilt. She cradled her portable phone on her shoulder while sorting through a stack of bikini panties.

"This is Maureen Callaway," came the voice. "I'm calling from CKWS Television to confirm the details for our charity fashion show."

"Yes of course, "Alice lied (she had completely forgotten). "Will you remind me date and time again, please, and confirm what you wanted us to model?"

"It'll be a live broadcast, two weeks from Monday, April 22nd, at our studio on King. You'll be going on at 8:30, and we would like you to model four different styles of thongs," Maureen continued. "One final point," she said, "we're showcasing local talent this year, staff and relatives. No professional models please."

"OK, that's great!" the clothier exclaimed—louder than she intended. After hanging up, she went back to her ruminations. "Thongs are getting more popular now. We should be able to sell a bunch, especially to college kids."

Alice's mind was whirling. They desperately needed to boost business. "What an opportunity, we could show our new line of beach wear; get a leg up on the competition. My staff, my relatives on live TV, showcasing our stuff, no cost. It's a win-win. This is too good to pass up."

As Alice hung up the phone, she inspected the ribbon of scarlet cloth in her hand. "This one will do nicely." Their new line was a bit more sensual and daring, blurring the boundary between what was suited for the beach and what belonged in the bedroom.

"Who was that?" As Bonnie came wandering over, she had a careful smile on her face, the one she got when she wasn't sure if Alice was talking to her or to herself.

"Oh nothing... nothing you have to worry about, I'll be taking care of this one, "she snapped. Alice was determined to reap the full rewards herself. This was her opportunity to shine. She could single-handedly save the business and her reputation in one fell swoop, and she could at the same time prove to Bonnie that she could market herself and the shop.

This could make the difference between solvency and bankruptcy.

Thoughts of the fashion show filled her every waking moment for the rest of the week. Who could she get to model? What style of thongs would be best? What colors?

And she only had two weeks!

Alice was no shrinking violet; she was a strong, educated, intelligent woman, and she could do this. She was a professional, and she was going to prove it.

Cayman Clothiers was a West Wing of commotion as Alice and anyone else vaguely akin to relatives or staff was lured in to get ready for the show. Alice searched far and wide, and even went to Heritage Canada to try to discover her distant relatives and follow them up to today. Even Bonnie had gotten over her lip and was on board, searching for appropriate candidates to model the thongs. Finding models was the first order of business, followed closely by the selection of suitable thongs that fit them. At first none of the prospective models were enthused with the thought of exposing themselves, with all their dimples and cellulite, on live television in front of thousands of viewers. But, finally, with much cajoling and not a few proffered gifts and concessions, two of her part-time salesgirls (university students and competitive swimmers) along with Bonnie's sister (a yoga instructor), with a little trepidation, agreed to be part of the show. Bonnie herself refused to even consider it.

One more model had to be found. Alice scoured all her sources for a relative or anyone remotely connected to the store who had relatively shapely hindquarters—without success. She went back two years on her payroll records to try to find a suitable candidate. An out-of-town third cousin was available, but not approved as not local enough talent by the hosting station.

Attempts to recruit the mail carrier and the meter maid (both fit and attractive young women) were in vain; they both laughed hysterically at the suggestion that they prance around the stage in the buff, no matter how Alice assured them that they were just beautiful and could probably score wealthy husbands or modelling contracts from the work.

By midweek, Alice started to panic. The fourth model had not materialized.

The moments before show time was ticking by, much faster than she anticipated with every movement of the classy antique clock up above the rows of clothes. With each passing second, she became more anxious.

After not a few sleepless nights, Alice conceded; she must model herself. At thirty-five, she had graduated from single-digit sizes. But her skin was relatively smooth, thanks to expensive lotions, exfoliations, and regular waxing, and she'd inherited her maternal grandmother's magical skin that never marred itself with a stretch mark. No, she wasn't as firm as she'd been in her younger years, but she maintained her curvaceous figure by working out regularly, walking her golden lab Echo twice a day, and restricting her diet to mostly organic food that her husband called hippie grub. "I like you with a bit of flesh on you," Brian often said, with a feigned look of lechery mimicking Denny Crane.

She could do it; she was up to the challenge. She was Model Number Four.

Now, Alice was even more determined to take a leadership role. It was their first fashion show and she'd convinced them to model. She scoured through fashion magazines and Internet articles and researched everything she could get her hands on about walking on runways, lighting, colours, and makeup. Their show had to be perfect. They chose plain flesh-coloured bikini tops, ones that would keep their display from being obscene and not take attention away from the beauty of the thong bikini bottoms.

She put herself and the other models through relentless drills of a runway walk known as the bounce, a rather complicated manoeuvre that involved almost crossing one's leg over the other during the step. It emphasized a sway of the hips and rump that would beautifully show off the highlighted garment. After hours upon hours of teetering in painfully high heels, all four of the models had the walk down. They'd even timed out how to march onto the stage, each precisely six paces behind the other, a space that they believed would be ideal for showing each individual person without blending them together too much, but also show how Cayman Clothiers's pieces complimented one another. They would reach the end of the runway, spaced six paces apart, and do a slow spin in unison. Then they would take turns one by one at the end, posing and turning. It was all a rather intricate dance, but the overall effect was both sensual and dazzling.

Alice paid a fortune to her day spa to be open on Sunday evening to give her and the other models an after-hours wax (absolutely everything below the neck), along with exfoliating treatments on their butt cheeks for a healthy glow. Alice limped home afterward, grateful she hadn't sprung for the bleaching treatment on top of everything else.

And then it was the big day. Townsfolk promenaded through the Limestone city in numbers, soaking up the solar rays from a warm, enticing sun that promised more pleasant days ahead. Rivulets of ice and snow melt swished down the gutters. It would soon be summer. How better to usher in the vernal equinox than with a beach fashion show?

Of course, as fortune would have it, Monday was their busiest day ever at the shop. Some sort of international women's water polo championship was happening in Kingston, and apparently Cayman Clothiers was the place to purchase some local fashion.

Though Alice's blood pressure was rising, she delighted in every sale. Alice and the two clerks took turns through the day to run down the street to a salon to get their hair styled and glamour makeup put on. Bonnie's sister, coiffed and painted to perfection, showed up half an hour before closing, while sales were still hopping.

The last customer left fifteen minutes after closing. The four ladies dressed at the store, each of them slipping into their selected garments and covering themselves with a heavy coat. At 8:30 exactly, a breathless Alice entered the front door of the television studio followed closely by her fellow models, all of whom were walking normally after the previous day's hair-removal discomfort. A frantic Maureen met the quartet and rushed them to the stage at a near sprint.

"You're ready?" she gasped.

Yes, they were all ready.

Bright lights and camera flashes blinded Alice as she shrugged out of her coat and bolted onto the stage, the others behind her. She involuntarily tensed her butt to stop her cheeks from jiggling too much. A draft in the old building raised goose bumps on her winter-white flesh, but she could be confident that she was at least hair and dead-skin free.

Head held high, Alice marched out onto the runway, doing the bounce walk, her rear end swaying to perfection, showing off that gorgeous scarlet thong. She knew that her bikini top, like each of her fellow models', blended perfectly to her skin tone, giving the effect that the thong was really all she was wearing (aside from the stiletto heels). She could hear the gasps from the crowd.

They were perfect. Every step was in unison. Alice reached the end of the runway, hearing the others stop behind her. They did their spins under the flashing lights, each taking a turn in that complicated dance of steps and turns they'd choreographed to look every bit as good as a Parisian fashion house.

As they took their final poses, Alice grew chill. Instead of the thunderous applause she was expecting, there were a few lewd hoots echoing out, but mostly shocked, pregnant silence. She blinked against the flashes, finally really seeing the audience.

It was a diverse crowd ranging from children to the elderly.

When Alice looked back into the wings, she could see that Maureen's eyes were wide with horror, her hands clamped over her mouth.

For the first time, she looked above the stage. A huge white banner with big black lettering hung there, proclaiming its purpose to the world.

CKWS TV Beach Footwear Fashion Show.

Shoes and Thongs for All Ages.

The Sentry

Fleeting white triangles of sailboats bobbed and dipped, tacking into the brisk wind on the lake. Lake Ontario stretched in a glittering blue expanse, partially framed by several of the Thousand Islands. Gulls squawked shrilly overhead. The lush green hillside was dotted with hikers and picnickers, sheltering in the shade to escape the summer heat. Royal Military College towered nearby, with its giant Canadian flag flapping in the breeze. The Wolfe Island Ferry discharged its usual motley collection of patrons. All was as it should be.

The original Fort Henry had been a solid structure of log palisades and molded masonry parapets built by the British and designed to repel Iroquois, French or American attacks from the water side. The recently refurbished Fort was aesthetically more pleasing, and still quite authentic. From this vantage point, of his position, located in the best tactical spot, Jackie Winters, latest in a long line of generations of sentinels, surveyed all the strategic approaches from the lakeside.

Huge crumbling limestone blocks straddled a cobbled walkway which formed, a bower-like, entrance to the Fort. An archway extended for a dozen paces over a planked drawbridge covering a green, frog-filled moat. The inner courtyard combined nineteenth century artifacts and authentic looking re-creations completed by the summer staff.

A small wooden ammunition wagon built in the Fort carpenter's shop, the most recent addition to the artifacts collection, sat unobtrusively just inside the Fort entrance. The slight difference in shades of black paint, the result of different paint mixers brought on by a change of shift, was hopefully not yet apparent to the sergeant major.

At nineteen, Jackie was the youngest, and most recent, student selected for summer employment at the Fort. It was a prestigious position. Jackie had also been accepted for enrolment at Queen's that fall, and his summer earnings, he calculated, would nicely cover his tuition and dorm fees for most of the year. He wanted to pay his own way. His father, a history professor at Queen's, was very pleased with Jackie's attitude and proud of his only son's success. So much so, that he had promised to buy him a car of his own when school resumed for the fall semester.

Jackie's athletic frame stood proud and straight (although a bit self-conscious) in his guardsman's uniform. To ensure that he would impress the tourists, Jackie had spent painstaking hours meticulously preparing his uniform. He had carefully groomed his bearskin, buffed his knee-high boots to a gleaming shine, pressed his pants to a razor-sharp crease, and brushed his tunic, removing any blemishes that were common in the dusty Fort.

Sentries on duty at Fort Henry were required to stand at attention in full dress uniform, with musket, for one complete hour at a time. This was Jackie's very first shift, and he hoped he could bear standing for sixty long minutes, motionless. The sun was scorching hot; he estimated the temperature at thirty degrees at least, and after twenty minutes he felt it must be a Fahrenheit one hundred.

The tourist bus threaded its way up the winding road leading to the Fort. Straining his eyes as far to the left as they would stretch, Jackie followed its progress. He wished he could move his head, but he didn't dare. Sergeant Major Byron had warned him, "Don't talk, don't move, only breathe if you have to, and remember, if you feel yourself falling, fall to attention." Byron was a Regular Army veteran and would tolerate no mistakes. "If it doesn't move, paint it, if it moves, salute it!" was his favourite line.

"He fired three students last year," a fellow Guardsman had confided to Jackie. "One had committed the grave offence of sneezing."

About twenty-five assorted tourists disembarked from the bus. They ambled toward the Fort entrance where Jackie's post stood. Butterflies fluttered in his stomach as they approached. The sun's rays seemed to penetrate the top of his bearskin, searing into his skull. "My, he looks nice," commented one elderly lady. Jackie's spirits soared. "He looks like a dummy," her escort added. "Yeah, he looks like one of those mannequins you see at the Bay," another man said. Jackie's elation melted. His arm ached from the leaden weight of his musket pressed into his right shoulder.

When all the insufferable tourists had filed slowly past, and made their disparaging remarks, Jackie could relax, if only slightly. He felt strands of bearskin matted to his forehead from perspiration. The sweat must be soaking into his leather headband, and making it shrink, he thought. It seemed to squeeze his aching head, cutting off the circulation, like a tourniquet.

A fly droned near his left ear, circled twice, hovered around his right ear and then disappeared. Probably a transient resident on the pile of goat shit from the Fort mascot, Wilbur, who lived in a squat shack on the back slope. Goat shit duty came up about once every two weeks, and often more frequently for the junior members of the Fort Guard. Wilbur looked good dressed up in his finery during sunset ceremonies and added that little extra bit of bling to the rustic surroundings. But Wilbur was not good company. He stank, badly.

Jackie's scarlet tunic had heavy quilted lining and a high tight-fitting coatee collar. Wearing it in this heat was like being shrouded in a damp wool blanket. Pressure from the bearskin on his head and the collar pushing up on his chin seemed to crush his brain like an apple in a cider press. Claustrophobic suppression started to absorb him. The stifling enclosure of his uniform began to envelop him like a cocoon. Piercing sparks of midday sun stabbed into his pupils. His head began to revolve and reel....

Soft yelping noises came from directly below his eye level. Jackie lowered his glance to see a short rusty-haired boy of about seven. The leash in his left hand led down to what was either a small dog or an oversized rat. The boy's face was covered in splotches of light brown freckles. A toothless grin gave him a malevolent look. Carelessly holding a melting ice cream cone, the boy mischievously inspected the sentry before him. Jackie forced his attention, away from the urchin, and directly to his front.

The sentry's eyes smarted from the salty perspiration that oozed from under his bearskin. He couldn't see the boy. He hoped the little imp had found something else to occupy himself. Feeling pressure on his right leg, Jackie relocated him. Instinct told him that the little rapscallion was rubbing his ice-cream cone on Jackie's trousers. Nausea washed through him. After he had spent all that time working on his uniform, this little monster had ruined his appearance in just a few seconds.

His heart raced; his fists clenched. This kid deserved a quick lesson. But the sergeant major would fire him, and that would disappoint his father. Jackie quelled his urge to dismember the scamp. He stared straight ahead, unblinking, unmoving. Strands of damp bearskin tickled his eyes and the bridge of his nose.

A methodic thumping on his left boot startled him. He strained to look down, but could not quite see the little beast, pounding his carefully spit-shone boots with a pop bottle, ruining the mirrored shine.

Summoning all his discretion and restraining power, the sentry managed once more to remain motionless.

It was hot. His trousers, tailored from heavy serge, were double padded in the seat and waist, and acted like a corset, squeezing his mid-section. He was smothering inside his uniform.

A shrill voice interrupted his thoughts. "Come on, Jinks. That's it," the urchin ordered. Relief filled Jackie; the little beggar was leaving. Wishful thinking.

"That's it, do it right there," the boy continued.

"What the hell was he doing?" Jackie puzzled. A warm wet trickle on his right leg answered his question. The rat dog was pissing on his leg! Nausea washed through him, and the world began to blur.

"Hey, Winters, lad, snap out of it! Get a grip on yourself, "bellowed the sergeant major.

Jackie surveyed his surroundings through cloudy, blurred eyes. Had he blacked out?

"That's it. Just a little sun, eh, boy? You'll be all right; keep the head up now. Good show man."

Satisfied that Jackie was okay, the sergeant major continued his rounds.

Still swaying a bit, Jackie slowly regained his confidence and composure. Haunting thoughts of a boy and dog started to creep into his consciousness. Soft yelping noises came from directly below his eye level. He broke regulations and lowered his glance fully to see a short rusty-haired boy of about seven, with a dripping, melting ice cream cone in his right hand. The leash in his left hand led down to what was either a small dog or an oversized rat.

Recovering somewhat, Jackie disregarded regulations and fully inspected his uniform. His bayonet sparkled in the sun, his boots were still gleaming, and his trousers were clean and razor creased.

It was going to be a long day....

Caribbean Chemistry

It was an understatement to say that Hobartson Augustus Wedderburn III was less than totally devoted to the study of chemistry. His talents, it seemed, were far more suited to jocularity and riotous living, and there was a surprising amount of that to be found in Mount Allison University in Sackville, New Brunswick. Chasing women, drinking, and partying were his major pursuits with chemicals and protozoa well down on his priority list; somewhere behind laundry and putting out the garbage. But why not, he would probably never have to work, especially in the chemistry field, after he inherited his family business of a large and thriving Jamaican sugar plantation.

There wasn't a professor at Mount Allison who had ever had Hobartson in their class who wished to have him again. He was careless, inattentive, and occasionally disruptive in class. He broke hearts constantly, leaving a trail of female students and even teaching assistants (and a librarian) in tears and despair.

He had made many friends with his ingratiating free-spending ways and bubbly personality. It was rumoured that Hobartson Augustus Wedderburn Junior, our Hobartson's father, had sent him to university in Canada to get him out of the country. Apparently, he had several paternity suits and jilted brides chasing him around the Island.

Somehow, however, beyond the perception and belief of most of his classmates and all his professors, and most likely himself, Hobartson managed to survive academically until the final exams of his graduating year. His professors were convinced that he had bought his term papers on the internet and bribed someone at the school to get the answers to all tests and exams. They were convinced that Hobartson was a con artist or a crook at the very least.

Fortified with a stiff belt of strong drink (Jamaican rum, no doubt), he entered the examination hall with hundreds of other sullen faced examinees. His professors anticipated the event with nothing less than great glee. This was to be the coup de grâce. Hobartson had done little to endear himself to his instructors. He had treated his studies and academics in general with nothing less than dumb insolence bordering on contempt. He embarrassed his professors repeatedly with esoteric questions that he found in an ancient chemistry manual he picked up at a yard sale. But Hobartson was to realize his just desserts at last. The day of reckoning had finally arrived. He could now be officially drummed out and sent back to his plantation in Jamaica to face the jilted brides and paternity suits. His instructors were ecstatic.

The final exams were held in a large gymnasium with dozens of rows of desks for different subjects. Hundreds of stressed out students shuffled in and sat dumb in anticipation of their scholastic guillotining. The atmosphere was tense. Only Hobartson seemed to have a frivolous look on his face. As far as he was concerned it would be party time that night, so let's get this perversion over with.

However, when Hobartson sat down and turned his exam paper over, he was visibly distraught. His normal glued-on little-boy, grin turned to an expression somewhere between alarm and dismay. He waved his hand furiously to attract the attention of the invigilator and started to gibber in fitful exasperated tones:

"I, I, think I'm having optical illusions or something!" Hobartson cried out as the professor in charge wandered over, with a derisive smirk on his face, to see what the commotion was all about.

The stern-faced professor invigilating the chemistry exam, who knew Hobartson's antics well, was neither amused nor impressed at this interruption. "You're not feeling well Mr. Wedderburn?" he asked, apparently not keeping the hopeful note out of his voice.

"This exam paper appears to be all Greek to me!" Hobartson lamented.

The professor looked down at him with the look of disdain that he reserved for his most inept students. He snatched the paper from Hobartson and brought it to eye level with a practiced flourish. His face then broke into an uncharacteristic wide grin as he announced to the assembled multitude:

"It is Greek! Mr. Wedderburn! You're in the wrong row!"

In the end, Hobartson did indeed ace his exam, and to this day nobody knows how he did it.

Benjie

It had been an eclectic day. Millie Jackson found herself locked in a pitch-black room about the size of a normal bathroom. She was alone in the deafening silence; all she could hear was the scrabbling of small animal claws and the rhythmic breathing of a giant young man standing within arm's reach.

She was terrified.

Her morning was typical and uneventful until her eight-year-old son Alexander came into the picture. Her husband George had left for work on time, but Alexander was running late. He hurriedly darted about trying frantically to finish his morning chores. These included letting Harlowe, their nine-year-old Golden Lab out in the back yard for his morning constitution along with feeding, watering, and cleaning the cage of his pet gerbil, Benjie. Harlowe was tall and handsome, but dumber than a bag of hammers, something like Scooby-Doo of television cartoon fame. Benjie was shorter and seemed to be smarter, but not much to look at, with his fuzzy, squat, hedgehog look.

Alexander tore through the kitchen, grabbed a pop tart for breakfast, slammed the screen door behind him, and sprinted head-long, his shirt tail hanging out, to catch the school bus. Alas, Millie could relax on the back deck with her morning cup of coffee.

However, she realized, shortly after she sat down, that something was amiss. Harlowe came running toward her excitedly, wagging his tail furiously, with something squirming in his mouth. A flipping, flapping pink protuberance wiggling like a worm, protesting being speared on a fisherman's hook, revealed that Harlowe had captured something, a small rodent perhaps, and seemed determined to swallow it. After sizing up the situation with not a little revulsion, Millie realized that Harlowe could choke to death.

"Why me?"

What to do? What to do? Millie racked her brain. She decided quickly to get a towel to try to pry the rodent from Harlowe's jaws while avoiding being bitten by his massive maw. Then as she ran past Alexander's room, she noted, to her horror and consternation, that Benjie's cage was open and Benjie was nowhere to be seen. Harlowe was eating poor Benjie!

What to do? What to do? Millie thought with added urgency now that Benjie was also involved in this crisis. With both Harlowe and Benjie in peril, she reflected, there might be a double funeral at the pet cemetery.

Having had some St John's Ambulance first aid training, Millie leapt into action like Wonder Woman (without the benefit of tights, cape, and superpowers).

Millie jumped behind Harlowe and straddling him, she grasped him tightly around the chest in Heimlich Maneuver fashion and squeezed and shook him as hard as she could. He was heavy, but she managed to give him some good jolts.

About the third heave, Harlowe choked and retched and gagged—a loud and sickening noise—and spit Benjie out flying across the room more than ten feet. Benjie skittered across the wooden floor and did several forward and backward summersaults. He finally came to a halt and lay there limply, not moving, wet and slimy from Harlowe's abundant saliva glands. Was Benjie dead?

Sobbing, Millie picked him up and gently placed him in a Tim Horton's Timbits box (the ones with the handle that made a good casket for small animals), which she lined lovingly with a couple of Kleenex. Even dead, poor Benjie should be comfortable.

Just as she was starting to plan the funeral, she heard a scratching sound coming from Benjie's casket. She looked in and saw that his little pink tail was moving slightly, and his little claws were scratching at the bottom of the box.

"He's alive!" she shouted, with the same exuberance that Dr. Frankenstein exhibited when he determined that his monster was alive.

Dark clouds were gathering as a thunder storm approached. Paying no attention to atmospheric conditions, Millie jumped in her Ford SUV and rushed to the vet's office with the casualty in hand. Literally and figuratively.

This is how she got locked in the normal bathroom sized dark room with the sound of a small animal scrabbling and a giant standing next to her within arm's length.\

The small animal was Benjie, of course, and the large young man next to her was a GI Joe type army sergeant, very tall with enormous broad shoulders and a coal-scuttle jaw with a cleft chin like a movie actor. He could easily pass for John Wayne or Clint Eastwood if you dressed him up in cowboy gear.

Just minutes before, at about 1000hrs, Millie and the sergeant had to park at P4, four levels below the vet's office and the Recruiting Centre, both located on the first floor of a high-rise office building.

The small room, of course, was the elevator that they took up four levels. It was pitch black because that approaching thunder storm had caused a power outage which in turn stopped the elevator, killed the lights, and briefly stranded its occupants.

Millie was a little confused and frightened at first, but quickly regained her composure when she remembered that she was with one of her Majesty's Canadian Army's finest. He would know what to do if they were stuck. She had nothing to fear; she was in good hands (be all you can be, and all that).

Finally, after what seemed to be hours, minutes probably, the power came back, the lights flickered on, and the elevator lurched upward to its destination. When it stopped on the first floor, Millie quickly exited the door and started toward the vet's office.

The sergeant, ramrod straight, with his coal scuttle cleft chin, called out to Millie in a deep baritone voice.

"Ma'am."

Millie turned quickly and faced him, somewhat surprised. Nobody had ever called her Ma'am before; she was undecided whether this was good or not.

"Yes," she answered in an urgent tone.

The Sergeant's serious military demeanor turned instantly into a broad boyish grin, showing off his straight, porcelain white teeth.

"Ma'am," he repeated, in an even deeper baritone, "Your Timbits are trying to escape."

Bear Facts

It was one of those torrid, humid, sticky Sunday afternoons in August. The temperature was wavering at the 30-plus mark. Our barbecue guests had all arrived, even the perennially late one, George Bond (no relation to James), who prided himself on keeping people (lesser mortals) waiting. Now, the hub-bub of suburban middle-aged (I hate that term) socializing could begin. After everybody had their drinks, and clusters of harried humanity gathered on the deck and flagstone patio, pseudo-serious discussion and small talk began in earnest. Even the taciturn amongst us joined in.

As usual, in this group, of pressured parents supporting an average of two and a half kids per family, it wasn't long before the conversation turned to offspring. An agitated conversation about orthodontists and braces and the cost thereof and necessity therefore began in one foursome and rippled up the deck stairs, to the top, and back down to the patio again. This was most evident amongst the dubious denizens held hostage by the burgeoning dental profession, up there with the banks and financial institutions in pressuring funds from the hapless public.

"We're out over $5,000 for Tiffany's first session," one matronly-looking mom in orange pedal pushers commented. "Just for a retainer and braces on her top teeth."

"Yeah, right," her husband added cynically, "she should have got a whole new head for that, wouldn't you think?" As an afterthought, he mumbled to nobody, "they'll be transplanting heads before long; they can replace just about every other body part now. I guess you'd want to get one with good teeth."

After this parental patter about bicuspids and overbites, the conversation turned to the all-consuming appetite of the average budding adolescent.

"Our three boys are eating us out of house and home," a bespectacled schoolteacher lamented. "It's like a Great White Shark feeding frenzy at our house."

"She's not kidding," her better half, a rotund man with spindly legs piped up. "A flat of of pop has a life span of two days. A four-litre tub of ice cream is lucky to last till sundown. It's really bad; they're like piranhas!"

Before long the major subject changed to what their little darlings were going to do when they grow up. The whole gamut of trades and professions was quickly covered from doctor to lawyer, to engineer and chartered accountant. The favourite trades were plumber and electrician, with IT person as a close runner up. There was also honourable mention of working in the geriatric care field which was ballooning with the average baby boomer getting past the retirement age and into the senior citizen ranks.

"A plumber makes as much money as a doctor," one father with a rakish handlebar moustache added, "and he doesn't have to pay a fortune to buy a bunch of specialist tools and equipment; at least they charge more!" All the other patriarchs within ear-shot nodded sagely Just about everybody had plans for their offsprings' future except one visibly morose dad with a permanent pressed on scowl like Churchill.

"What's your son going to be when he grows up?" someone asked. The man signed deeply and muttered, "An octogenarian, I think." A polite ripple of laughter – not too loud for appearance sake, burst out from the bystanders.

Finally, before the hamburgers, bratwurst, baked potatoes, and Caesar salad were served, the inevitable subject of leaving the nest came up. It appeared that most parents, especially fathers, were for it. "The sooner the better," two men, at both ends of the group, said in unison, smiling broadly at each other, with a thumbs-up approval.

"We sent our son off to college last year," a proud father in loud purple and yellow Bermudas volunteered. "Because we figured he had a head on his shoulders," he added almost as an afterthought.

"By the looks of his marks," the boy's mother quipped with a wrinkled smile, "he must have a different head on his shoulder every night! We only hear from him when he wants money."

"Fortunately, he hasn't brought any of these girls home yet", the yellow Bermudas surmised."

"Oh, our daughter emails regularly," another mom added proudly. "And texts. I've learned how to use emojis now."

"My son doesn't seem to want to do anything productive," a depressed-looking mother said. "Since he graduated from high school, he just flops around the house, playing games on the computer, working for little bits at minimum wage when he wants something and can't squeeze the money out of us."

"We're trying to figure out how to motivate him and get him to accept some responsibility," the frustrated father added. If he were to move out and have to fend for himself, he'd have to mature in a hurry."

The depressed-looking mother nodded vigorously.

A minuscule little professor of biology, from Queens University, with a neatly trimmed beard and, pale white skinny legs, then jumped into the discussion. "The higher primates such as gorillas, baboons and chimpanzees teach their offspring to survive in the cruel world of the jungle." He recited in a practiced lecture voice. "Domesticated animals such as cows, sheep, pigs and even chickens teach their young how to survive predators in the barnyard and foraging pasture fields. The larger mammals that we are more familiar with in Canada such as bears, for instance, teach their cubs everything they must know to look after themselves in the wild. And then one day after about six months, when they're convinced that the young ones can survive, they sound the danger alarm and the cubs in a pre-arranged drill, climb a tree as quick as they can."

A crowd started to gather around the learned professor, listening intently. "The mother bear then runs away and leaves the cubs to their own devices in the wilderness."

There was a collective gasp.

"The poor little things," the mother in orange pedal pushers moaned.

"The cub may stay up the tree for days, but finally he gets the message and comes down. And, at last, he's really on his own, and has to fend for himself" the professor said triumphantly with a flourish of his wine glass.

"There's only one problem" the dad with the recalcitrant son added. "The tree in my back yard isn't big enough to hold my son!"

With almost a minute of uproarious laughter, the listening audience gave him a standing ovation (since they were all standing, this took little effort). Acknowledging their applause, the dad made a deep exaggerated bow, took a step backward, and promptly fell over the rail of the deck and onto the fortunately, soft garden below.

He lay there on his back, longer than he had to, covered with sticky, black earth and manure, and got up faster than he had to, and headed for home and the shower.

"Is this how your son does it?" an erstwhile taciturn observer asked.

He didn't answer.

Part 3

A World with Whimsy

Toby Quick

Call me Ichabod.

I works in the Yablonski Brothers' sardine factory in Yarmouth.

My best friend in the front-line scaling, gutting, and packing department is Quakwai (pronounced Quack like a duck and weigh like weigh yourself), a behemoth Mig Maw fellow from Cape Breton, covered with tattoos and piercings. He even has a bolt-type thing punched through his tongue—if you can imagine that. Folks say he got the tattoos in Dorchester prison in New Brunswick; I rather hope not—that would hurt some fierce.

At first, he scared the bee jeepers out of me, but turns out he was right friendly, even kind. He seemed to take to me for some reason, and some Saturday nights in days gone by when he was too drunk to drive, he would let me drive his ancient Chevy into town. Often, we was put in jail over night because of some misdemeanor that Quakwai set to happening. He liked to fight, especially white fellows, of which there was a whole lot in Yarmouth.

Our floor boss for the night shift was Aloishes Abner. When I first met him, the stone-hard look on his face set me cold. He was a mean-looking man with great big cauliflower ears (had both of those), and only one eye, one arm, and one leg. He sported a black patch over his left eye (which was glass), and he would take out the marble in front of his workers at lunch time just to gross them out and put them off their grub, which they would shove aside and then he would gobble up. He was not a pretty sight—he even scared Quakwai, though he would never admit it.

Abner was also fitted with a shiny stainless-steel hook on his right arm which he used to open selected sardine cans for inspection with a quick twist of the hook. It was kind of scary to watch him in this daily ritual. The hook was a freaky-looking thing, and Boss relished flashing it about, like Zorro with his sword, just to scare the pants off anyone standing near. His missing leg was replaced by a crude wooden peg, rather than a proper fake leg, and nobody had the stones to ask why. Health Canada ain't perfect, but they normally ain't that cheap.

The one advantage to him having a peg leg is that we could hear him coming, the wood stumping on the floor. We said that to one another often as sort of a consolation. When Boss discovered this, he tied rags round the peg to muffle the sound so's he could sneak up on the long-suffering night shift workers, to try to catch them napping or slacking off.

Of course, my friend had something to say about that. "Boss is ugly, right, but he's a hand-on type and keeps an eye on us at all times."

Sometimes Quakwai could be funny.

Boss Abner ruled his men as though the steel hook were the iron hand of Stalin. His self-appointed duty was to make sure that the sardines were packed properly, with the tails on the left side facing out and the tails on the right facing in. And if it weren't done that way he was sook, and who ever cocked it up was some sorry.

Things don't stay the same for long in life, and it was true here. Trouble was brewing off the coast, and of course Abner was gonna get himself up in the middle of it.

A giant speckled seal, thought to have been dropped in secret by our competitor, Leblanc's in New Brunswick, was eating all the offshore sardines that ought to have been harvested by Yablonski's in the local fishing grounds.

"If this keeps up, the factory might have to close." That were the rumour, and it floated round the day and night shifts.

"Not on my watch!" Boss Abner roared. "I been here since I was low to Young John Pike's age."

Quakwai cocked his head at me. "A teenager," I says.

"Back when they was still driving horses 'stead of cars," Quakwai whispered, too quiet for Boss Abner to hear him. He'd learned after the peg leg incident.

It would be a sad day if Yablonski's had to close, not only for the employees, but for all the townspeople who depended on the factory. Now, me, I'se just a Bluenoser hardly been to school but I knows what a factory does for a town. Town lives and dies on it. I could see Yarmouth as a ghost town, like many other former fishing villages on the North Shore, boarded up due to the depletion of the fish stocks.

After another day of low yield, Boss Abner was pacing and shouting profanities, and most of us wsd just staying out of his way. He rained down threats and curses on the seal, to the point where we wasn't sure if he were talking about the devil or an ocean creature.

It was a deep and vicious hatred, really too much for what it was. It's life by the water, right, sometimes there's no fish. It wouldn't be the seal's fault... it was just doing what seals did. Sure, it had to be took out, but for Abner... it seemed... personal.

"It's what happened, you know," Quakwai told me. "To Boss. The seal bit off his arm and leg. Poked out the eye with the tip of his flipper."

"What about the ears?" Boss's cauliflower ears were rather something.

Quakwai shrugged. "Fight, most likely. Big fellows like me, we can make it hurt."

Boss Abner put up an award of $1,000.00 cash for anyone who seen the giant seal off the wharf. The first worker to sight the spotty bastard known as Toby Quick, because of how fast he could move and escape, would have the money.

"How's he manage to get that kind of scratch together?" someone asked, as we was hunched over our smokes at break. It were't like we was turning much of a profit these days—Boss had been shortening shifts just so's nobody got laid off.

Quakwai grinned round his hand-rolled 'cigarette' that we all could smell wasn't filled with tobacco. "Bet he sold his glass eye."

Starbum and Tubbs, Abner's two subordinate supervisors on the night shift, chuckled. They was a burly-looking pair with dull eyes who both answered to both names. Young John Pike called them "Rosencrantz and Guildenstern," though none of the rest of us knew what that meant. But Young John had been to a half year of university upalong somewheres, which is a sight more'n anyone else there.

"Boss is going nuts," Tubbs said quietly, even though Abner was out on the wharf. "He don't think about nothing else... I think he's gone a bit tetched."

Starbum nodded. "I been tellin' him that b'y's a menace, but he don't care. You can't bother talkin' to him 'bout it... best not try."

Through the smoky darkness, I could see the bruise on Starbum's cheek.

Over the next few weeks, Boss would stride along the wharf, night and day, fair weather and foul, stomping along the deck, with his wooden leg thumping on the boards, stabbing his hook viciously into the rails with each stride, looking for the elusive Toby Quick. For miles around, anyone with decent ears could hear the *thwack! Thwack! Thwack!*

So we all kept giving him a wide berth. "Crazier than a jaybird," Quakwai would say, before lighting another joint.

I'd always give him the same response. "Maybe you should give him one of those."

A few of the guys grinned, but we all knew it wouldn't happen. Nobody wanted to get on his bad side—if he had a not-bad side. The rest of management even noticed, and they was all lunatics themselves.

So yeah, it finally happened like we all knew it would.

One grey, overcast day, the Seal with its tell-tale speckled hum back, was spotted near the wharf, greedily gobbling up all the sardines in his path like a giant vacuum. Every sardine he chomped wouldn't come out of the water, wouldn't go in the cans, and wouldn't bring us no money.

"Well, come on, then!"

Boss Abner come scrambling by, his double-barrel 12-guage in his hand, his hook waving wild enough so's we was ducking out of the way. "In the dory!"

Me and Quakwai didn't take time to protest. We got our arses in there and took the oars. "Come a daisy!" Abner roared.

"You loaded properly?" Maybe I shouldn't have asked, but I seen a shotgun misfire before, and it ain't pretty.

"Buckshot."

Good enough.

As we skims across the water, I seen the flapping flipper of the seal as it dove and lurched, hungrily sucking back hundreds of our tiny fish in a single gulp.

"You done now, b'y! Fillin' your boots with our fish! Not no more!"

Abner took aim and fired, but faithful to his name, Toby Quick was gone. Course he tries a few more times, but it ain't so easy using a shotgun with one proper arm and a hook, right, so nothing hit.

The seal floated along, doing the back stroke, almost like this show was meant to entertain him. He chattered, and there were no mistaking it... he were mocking Abner.

"Fuckin' beast!" Abner shot again. And again.

His ammunition finally expended, the threw his gun at the seal, just missing him.

I never seen a face so red before. He was livid, his face like the taillights of a car on a dark night... might've been actually was foaming at the mouth.

Then I seen the look in his eye. "Boss, no!"

I lunged, but I missed.

He was blind, I think, in his rage. "Fuckin' whore-born beast!" He jumps into the water, right at the seal, steel hook flashing.

The water thrashed and swirled, and I could see him wrapped round the still-chattering thing. Lightning lit the sky and I could see his face for a flash, patch gone, eye gone, a blank, grotesque hole left to gape.

Then he goes under, and there's red in the water.

Three times more, he lurched up, shrieking and flapping. Last time, blood and foam coming from his mouth. Me and Quakwai, we can't do nothing but sit in the boat.

Then he don't come back up at all. Just a swirl of blood and a floating log... no, his peg leg.

Not sure how long we sat there, me and Quakwai, but at some point we rowed over and grabbed the peg and brought it with us back to shore.

And that was that. Boss was never seen again. And the sardines come back, lots and lots. Abner must have killed the seal, or at least gave him enough of a puck that he lot for better waters.

They never found his body, so they just buried the peg. In death, he were bigger than in life. We all gathered round the grave, everyone having something good to say.

"The finest kind."

"Yablonski's poster boy."

"He were a legend, he were."

Quakwai just stood there and cried.

Body weren't in the ground three days when the grave was robbed. Leg was gone. The constabulary blamed rowdy teens, but those of us at Yablonski's, we knows the truth.

Now, when the rain's pouring down and it's blowing a gale round Yarmouth, you sees the gauzy figure of Boss Abner marching along the wharf walkway, stomping his wooden leg down with each step, stabbing his hook into the rails.

And yeah, no matter how much the blow, you hears the *thwack! Thwack! Thwack!*

The Tire Man

The sign spelled out in big red letters, "Giovanni's Firestone—Flats Fixed While You Wait." The bicycles of laughing children littered the pavement in front of the shop. A grinning bear of a man moved deftly from bike to bike like a chief surgeon in an ER trauma centre.

"Hey, Frankie," the man commented to a cherubic boy of about seven with his two front teeth missing, "be a little more careful next time, dont'a hit the curb." The boy nodded politely. "Yes, Mr. Colombo. Thank you ver' much for fixin' my bike. Got a spelling test today."

"Good luck on that," the man returned. "Spellin's a tough thing... never learned it well myself. But you can; you just work hard. Watch the cars, now."

Just as the man was about to repair the sixth bicycle that morning, a waving, frantic owner pulled up in a red, late-model New Yorker. The vulpine-faced Giovanni stepped out with his alligator shoes. "Fabio, how many times I tell you? Huh?" he wailed, slapping his forehead. "We no fix the bicycle for free! It's a not a good business!"

Fabio sauntered sullenly back into the garage. "It don't cost nothing for a few patches and a little glue." Giovanni would take it out of his wages, he knew, but he didn't much care.

Fabio Giuseppe Colombo was the tire man at Giovanni's Firestone. The shop was strategically sited at the corner of Steele and Avenue Road. A huge tractor tire out front made it something of a local landmark. For years, area residents had been giving directions to go "past the big tire" or "if you pass the big tire, you've gone too far."

Fabio was short and squat, with wide, turned-out feet that made him walk like a duck. Black, curly hair flowed out from both sides of his Andy Capp leather hat, making him look not unlike a very large woodchuck. The tire man's squabby feet were shod in black rubber boots with red piping around the toes. Giovanni, the owner and brother-in-law, purportedly kept him on at the shop out of family loyalty. But, if the truth be known, Giovanni made good money from Fabio's expertise at fixing tires. "The tire man can fix any flat," Giovanni often boasted, with a look of avarice on his face. And although he complained about the bike tires, those customers tended to grow up to eventually bring their cars to the shop. Fabio's generosity was building loyalty. But Giovanni, who would squeeze a nickel so hard the beaver would shit, still took the cost of the bike tire supplies from Fabio's wages.

The tire man's enthusiasm for his tires was legend. He would line them up in order of size, by height, width and white wall or black wall-type. Plugs and patches and cans of cement and glue were positioned strategically on his bench, all ideally placed for quick action.

Fabio had one passion, however, that overshadowed his tires. After work, all his energies were devoted to professional hockey. Fabio was a Maple Leaf's fanatic. His favourite players were the goalies and the area above his work bench was wallpapered with posters of such luminaries as Turk Broda, Terry Sawchuck, and Johnny Bower. Fabio even bought an old set of pads and a second-hand face mask so that he could play goal with his son, Luigi, and the neighbourhood kids at their local outdoor rink.

Fabio loved his job as tire man. But, without his powerful arms and hands, he'd never survive. "Fabio has a hand like a baseball mitt," one regular customer would often say.

"Ya, und fingers like der bratwurst," a German patron often quipped.

After years of handraulic effort, Giovanni (thinking he could make more money) was grudgingly convinced to buy Fabio an automatic tire changer and vulcanizing machine. Characteristically, Giovanni refused to pay the extra fifty bucks for assembly, so the task fell to Fabio. Instructions were included, but Fabio soon grew impatient and assembled the contraption on his own initiative. At last it was together (so to speak). Fabio reached over and stuck the heavy three-pronged plug in the wall socket. An arcing blue flame shot from the vulcanizing machine up Fabio's arm and through his huge frame. He shook and glowed effervescent for eternal seconds before he wrenched himself loose. The tire man fell in an exhausted lump to the cement floor. He hollered feebly for help until Giovanni finally came back from his ornate office and got him to the hospital.

"Those big rubber boots probably saved your life." the doctor told Fabio matter-of-factly. "It's a good thing you're so big too, or you never would have survived the shock."

After an afternoon's rest, Fabio was back to his tires. The new vulcanizer seemed no worse for wear after Giovanni reluctantly had the company put it together right, but Fabio was not the same. He felt a surging energy course through his body and inexplicably pieces of rubber were attracted to him like metal filings to a magnet. Once, even, a fist-sized scrap of rubber flapped up and hit him in the chest. Fabio was dumbfounded (and not just a little embarrassed) and afraid of his strange new affliction.

The next weekend, however, he discovered an advantage to his rubber woes. While playing scrub hockey with Luigi and the kids, the tire man found that all their shots were attracted to his body. The shots on the ice would hit his feet and the low shots would bounce off his knee pads. Even one blistering slap shot, which appeared to be a sure goal, mysteriously hit him in the middle of his belly pad. Fabio was attracting the pucks to his body. Whenever he placed himself in the net, nothing got by him. This phenomenon drew great attention from local hockey fans. Eventually Fabio's strange talent drew the notice of a major-league scout named Butch Arnold. Arnold watched in controlled awe as burly players tried in vain to score on the "Fabulous Fabio".

The scout waded through the throng of admirers and sidled up to Fabio. “How would you like to try stopping some shots in the big league?” he offered a stunned tire man.

“Sh, sh, sure a would,” Fabio stammered.

Arnold got the prospective goalie’s number, gave him an embossed Leaf’s business card and was gone.

The next Tuesday Fabio got the call from Arnold. “Can you come to practice tomorrow morning at ten?”

“Not ‘til after work at six,” Fabio answered absently.

“I’ll fix it,” Arnold returned, business-like. The scout was good to his word. The next morning, Giovanni told his tire man that a big hockey boss had called and offered free tickets if Fabio could practice with the team. Giovanni was impressed.

When Fabio showed up at the Gardens, a confident, grinning Arnold met him and took him to meet Toe Imlaw, the head coach of the Maple Leaf’s.

“Toe, this is Fabio Colombo, the goalie I was telling you about.”

The great coach stuck his hand out. “Nice to see ya here, Mr. Colombo. Let’s see what ya got.”

Fabio wasn’t sure what to say.

“Let’s get dressed,” Butch offered, leading Fabio to the dressing room.

“You can’t wear that stuff!” the scout scoffed as Fabio unloaded his antiquated, worn-out gear on the floor. “They’ll drill holes in you.”

“Spike!” he hollered. “Get a set of goalie kit for Mr. Colombo here.”

The trainer inspected the tire man. “Ain’t got a set big enough,” he mumbled to himself. But after much straining and tugging, Fabio was strapped into a brand-new set of pads. “This stuff smells like a new caddie” the tire man quipped.

“Get out there and do your stuff,” was all Arnold said.

All eyes were transfixed as the tire man made his entry. He fell twice in a heap before reaching the blue line and then slipped unceremoniously into the net feet first. "Didn't know I had to wear skates," Fabio lamented to a flustered scout.

"Just stand in the middle!" Arnold snapped to jeers of laughter. Imlaw was at the bench, head buried in his arms, wailing something about "Why me?" Then he finally looked up.

"Maharovich!" he yelled, rolling his eyes toward the net. "Take a few shots at Butch's new discovery there!" he said, with a stifled look of derision, "Try not to kill him!"

Big Hank Maharovich skated over with a cocky smirk on his face. "What if I break him?" he asked winking at Imlaw. The Big M whirled down the ice, stick handling methodically. Just short of the blue line, he rifled a wrist shot that caught a squatting, unmoving Fabio in the right shoulder. His second attempt bounced off the tire man's knee pad and a third with rebound careened off Fabio's chest and skate respectively. The Leaf's top scorer sulked off into the corner shaking his head.

"Moose!" Imlaw roared, "put one past him." The hulking defenceman charged at the goal like a locomotive. He skated to within ten feet, dexterously moving the puck from side to side and shifting his weight to try to get Fabio to make the first move. The tire man stood his ground - unmoving (to be honest, if the truth be known) not having a clue what to do.

Moose finally took his shot from about six feet, a blazing wrist shot about four inches off the ice, expertly aimed at the open right corner. Inexplicably, the shot careened and bounced off Fabio's left leg just above the ankle. Spontaneous applause erupted.

Imlaw was convinced.

The practice continued with Fabio at one end and Furor, of Oilers fame, in the opposing net. The final score was a lopsided 6–0. The tire man had been peppered with dozens of high-velocity shots, yet not one had gone in.

Imlaw was more than happy to sign the tire man. He was delighted at Fabio's terms. All he asked was $100.00 for each game he played and free seats for his family and friends. His only other conditions were that he play only home games and that he be able to quit on twenty-four hours' notice. That way, Fabio rationalized, he wouldn't have to give up his job at Giovanni's. "You're a hard bargainer," Imlaw feigned, grasping Fabio's paw with both hands. Eagleman, the team lawyer, witnessed the contract with a look of diabolical anticipation. The dollar signs gleamed in his eyes as visions of television specials and merchandising danced in his head.

The initial reaction of Toronto fans was predictable. As the short, fat, rumpled apparition waddled timorously across the ice to take up his post in the Leaf's net against Montreal, the whole Gardens was aghast. Everybody thought it was a practical joke. Their mirth and disbelief, however, was quickly dissolved as the vaunted Canadiens, try as they may, were unable to score.

"Fabulous Fabio shuts out Canadiens" was the headline in the Sunday Star. The tire man was an overnight sensation. Five other teams were defeated in quick succession.

"Tire Man impenetrable," the Toronto Sun flashed across its front page.

"The Great Gronsky foiled again" the Globe headlined.

The opposition fell like so many dominoes. Fabio was a celebrity beyond his wildest dreams. Fans, admirers, and even curiosity seekers would line up for hours just to shake his hand and get his autograph. Fabio had hardly any time to fix his tires. But Giovanni wasn't complaining. His tire sales had never been better. Business was booming.

As Fabio's fame and fortune grew, so did his weariness. It wasn't simply his grueling schedule... something was wrong, he came to realize. The energy that once surged through him was wavering. His power to attract rubber was slowly trickling away.

Fabio was, in the end, a tire man. He knew that if there was a leak, it wouldn't stop until all the air was gone unless you could make a patch.

So late one night, after everyone else had gone home, he headed into the garage again to see what the vulcanizing machine could do for him. He fiddled with this, that, and the other thing, until he got that arc of blue surging through his body yet again. He held on until the world went black.

Turns out, that machine could stop his heart quite effectively. It was sheer dumb luck that an ambulance happened to be passing by on its way back to the fire station, and the two paramedics on board saw the flash of blue light.

Thanks to some CPR and a defibrillator, the tire man lived to walk out of the hospital three days later, broken ribs wrapped in tape, electricity burns daubed in ointment.

The next day, Imlaw shook his head sadly as Fabio left the coach's office. Eagleman was outraged, insisting it could just be an anomaly and the tire man's powers could come back. They could get scientists and engineers to help. Until then, they could capitalize upon his healing process, maybe make a regular show out of it. They could make a fortune!

But Fabio was determined, and a contract was a contract. He had given twenty-four hours' notice, as agreed, and he was relieved of all obligations to the Maple Leafs.

The huge tractor tire is still out in front of the Firestone tire shop at the corner of Steele and Avenue Road, but the sign now reads, "Fabio and Giovanni's Firestone."

Every morning, the bicycles of laughing children litter the pavement in front of the shop.

Frankie has had the highest grade in spelling in his school, three years running.

Part 4

Moments That Made Me Myself

Old Soldiers Never Laugh

I didn't want to be there. I'd rather have taken a month-long hike with full pack, after a high colonic, with no toilet paper, in a forest filled with poison ivy. I would have rather wandered naked through Somalia. I would have rather gone for a swim in shark-infested waters after I'd crawled through some barbed wire.

But I was here.

Then, I was an old soldier. Now, looking back on this time in my life, I'm an even older soldier. I'm long retired, but so many years in the Forces gives one an unshakeable identity that lasts even beyond the grave.

At the moment where this tale begins, I might very well have been near the grave. Years of alcoholism does that to a person. And I was at the point where I had two choices: quit or die. My body ached. My head ached. My thoughts were fascinating, a beautiful synchronicity of brilliance, but they were accompanied by so much pain and misery I couldn't bear them.

There was no turning back. The heavy self-locking doors, of Maplewood Addictions Treatment Center in Winnipeg Manitoba, clicked ominously shut behind me. I was committed for the duration; either these touchy feely, tree-hugging, pinko commie hippies would cure me, or I'd be thrown back to the mercy of my erstwhile companions, Jim, Jack and Johnnie—that would be Beam, Daniels, and Walker. And my companions would indeed, kill me.

But I wasn't going in passively. I marched in there with my head high, my back straight, my face impassive. I could hear laughter in the distance, and I frowned in disapproval.

I was a soldier. This was a solemn mission. I was going to take it seriously. I wasn't going to laugh. I never laughed.

A veteran of over forty years in the Canadian Army, my forte and my passion was reorganizing things. About five minutes after I got through the doors, I decided that this place was in dire need of revamping—by me. My thoughts shimmered and shone as the place took shape before me, rearranged into more efficient and effective shapes. Yes, I could do this.

I was determined to fix the place. I would overcome my alcoholism with the same stoicism I used to overcome all the other trials of my life. And I would leave Maplewood a better place in my brilliant wake.

Determination and destiny are two different things.

For my first few days, a nurse showed me around. She was an iron-jawed woman of middling years whose name never really registered on me. In my head, she quickly became Nurse Ratched. As I made my observations, she would counter them with explanations that I found to be as ridiculous as that of any bureaucrat.

There were lineups everywhere. We waited in line for pills; we waited in line for coffee; we waited in line to talk to our counselors; we waited in line to go walking; and we waited in line to come back from our walks. "If you stagger the arrival/departure times, the lines wouldn't nearly be so long," I pointed out.

Nurse Ratched frowned, her mouth pursing in a manner that reminded me of my Aunt Fanny (may she rest in peace). "Waiting in line teaches you patience. It also teaches you to tolerate discomfort. Both of those qualities are frequently in short supply for those with addictions."

"I was in the military; I've tolerated more discomfort than you could dream of."

She actually looked rather pleased at that. "Excellent. Then you won't have trouble waiting in line in accordance with the rules."

Maplewood had rules for everything. There were rules for eating, rules for sleeping, rules for showering, rules for sitting, rules for standing, and even rules for walking. Nurse Ratched explained them to me slowly, as if my alcohol-muddled brain might not be able to keep up with normal speech.

"May I at least empty my bowels as I choose to?" I asked.

She arched a brow. "You are to empty your bowels into a toilet, quietly. You will clean yourself afterward and flush. You will not clog the toilet or make any sort of mess. You will wash your hands before you leave the bathroom."

Each inmate had their own porcelain coffee cup inscribed with their name, which could be impounded by predatory staff if let out of sight of the owner. Beds had to be made just so, and no clothing was allowed outside the closet. Vacuuming, dusting and scrubbing the toilet, shower and sink were a mandatory daily ritual. Bedrooms and bathrooms had to be inspection-ready for most of the day.

"This seems so silly," I said.

"You're a soldier," Nurse Ratched countered. "You're used to rules and regulations."

"I'm used to rules and regulations that have a purpose. What does all of this minutia have to do with recovery from alcohol or drug addiction? How does hurry up and wait help me, or any of us?"

She wouldn't answer me.

Well, that was it. I was going to have to become McMurphy. My never surrender policy, garnered from my military service, and studying Winston Churchill clicked in.

"Dress is strictly regulated to be modest and in good taste.," Nurse Ratched explained. "We will chastise female patients for showing too much cleavage, for example."

The army has become a rather egalitarian place, and that has been my mindset for some years. Therefore, that rule seemed particularly sexist to me. So I offered what I thought was a simple solution to this problem.

"Rather than restricting the women from showing their cleavage, why not let the men wear their pants plumber style? This would quickly solve the cleavage conundrum. Women would soon be buttoned up to the neck in a campaign to ban all cleavage—male and female—after they witnessed a few hairy plumbers cleaves."

Nurse Ratched blinked once. Slowly. "What's wrong with you?"

"Wrong with me? You're the one ungrateful for my suggestion."

So we moved on to the pharmaceutical portion of the treatment program. This might very well have been the most inefficient pill dispensing operation in the universe. Two pill pushers sat behind a large horseshoe-shaped desk. First, they checked voluminous patient ledgers, leafing through them one at a time, and then handed out medication from small wicker baskets stored separately in large cupboard ten feet behind them. Each basket was fetched separately, and each pill was checked individually and then dispensed one at a time into a small plastic cup. If a mistake was made in the dispensing process, the whole pantomime was repeated, even slower. Ponderous and tedious, the operation was most tiresome and frustrating to the 100-plus patients who lined up for pills four times a day.

My suggestion, carefully recorded on foolscap, in pencil, to improve their accuracy and speed by using pill carts on wheels with color-coded, alphabetically marked drawers was not appreciated. I even showed them how to establish concurrent activity by starting at both ends of the alphabet and meeting in the middle.

I showed the plan to the pill pushers and to Nurse Ratched. They all stared at me, then went back to their duties. This was obviously too complicated for them to grasp.

"The wait," Nurse Ratched ground out through gritted teeth, "allows patients the opportunity to test their tolerance threshold."

And so it did; I was severely tested.

Next up was the dining room.

The rows of dining tables ran parallel to the serving counter, which restricted both traffic flow and failed to make the best use of space. "This needs to be completely turned around, both literally and figuratively. If rearranged perpendicular to the serving counter, both space and movement would be optimized."

Nurse Ratched didn't even answer me on that one. She took me to the cooks, who claimed their names were Larry, Mo, and Shirley. I didn't believe them. I figured they'd made that up just to see if we would laugh. But I didn't want to laugh. I wanted to fix this institution and get the hell out of it.

Larry, Mo, and Shirley listened to my suggestion, then told me that they were not interested in any changes, space saving, movement optimizing, or otherwise.

"So we just have to dine cheek by jowl after a slow procession of one way, one-sided cafeteria-style pickup of all food," I complained to Nurse Ratched.

"Think of the togetherness," she suggested.

Since when was togetherness more important than efficiency or ergonomics?

The compulsory daily walk for alcoholics, drug addicts and other afflicted souls, was next on my target list. In my naturally unbiased opinion, based on my experience in the Army, the daily constitutional, designed to improve fitness and morale, was neither safe nor secure, and due diligence was not practiced by the institution. I was not convinced that allowing scores of alcoholics and drug addicts, loose in the woodland trails, on their own for up to an hour at a time, in the woods, sometimes after dark, was a wise thing to do. Cell phones were not allowed, and no staff was present. What if we ran amok? Who would call 911 for assistance? What if one of the patients decided to climb a tree? Who would call the fire department? Why not send out two staff escorts, I opined, one at the front of the patient walking column and one at the back, armed with cell phones. This suggestion also fell on deaf ears.

"Daily walks," Nurse Ratched explained, "are designed to teach patients responsibility and allow for informal discussion of topics too intimate to be discussed inside. And after all, no serious problem have been encountered."

"Yet."

My suggestions were falling on complacent, apathetic ears. I began to wonder if I shouldn't organize a large-scale escape to demonstrate the relevance of my concerns—and the brilliance of my plans.

I didn't like not being heard. I was of a rather advanced rank, and I was used to being obeyed. Nurse Ratched, however, appeared to consider herself a general to my lieutenant-colonel. That was ridiculous. She'd never seen live combat in her life. How could she command me?

"Just accept the rules," she advised. "They are clear, concise, and always in your best interests. If you accept the rules and follow them, you will have a much better chance at success. Whatever situation arises, there will be a rule for how to handle it."

She explained to me the regulations for visiting. "Male inmates are not to grope their visiting wives or girlfriends, and females are forbidden to grope their visiting husbands or boyfriends. All dogs are to be kept on a leash at all times."

That seemed to me to be the pinnacle of pedantry.

"Those aren't entirely clear," I pointed out. "Could I grope my dog, or put my wife on a leash?"

I could see the flush rising on her neck. "The first of those is illegal," she snapped. "And as to the second... that is private between yourself and your wife at your own home. It does not happen here."

"Just so you know, that doesn't happen at home for me either."

She didn't appear to care.

My final critique concerned the lack of security in the complex itself. Despite the angry, intolerant and volatile nature of some of the patients, no formal security was deemed necessary. So I spent every spare moment I could with pencil and foolscap, trying to design the perfect security system. I didn't sleep at night. I sat and worked in my room. During the day, I sat in that inefficiently-designed dining room, working away.

In order to demonstrate the necessity of a new system, there would need to be... something. A demonstration. Perhaps a full-scale riot. So I began to plan that, along with the eventual security protocol that would prevent it from happening again.

Before I could decide whether my proposal should include guards armed with clubs, tasers or shotguns, Nurse Ratched marched in with two burly orderlies.

"You're planning a riot?" she asked me.

"Just to make a point," I assured her. "We won't actually damage anything. Too much." A few of the other patients that I'd discussed this with had seemed quite enthusiastic.

The three of them escorted me to the psychiatrist in what I thought was a rather rough and unceremonious fashion. As I stumbled along, being held up by those big men, I struggled to explain what I was doing, to describe those shimmering thoughts that whirled around me, but they wouldn't listen at all.

For four days, I endured tests and interrogations. Interestingly, I was spared from the lineups during this portion of my stay. I was hardly allowed to leave my room at all. So I stayed there, with my pencils and paper, drawing up endless plans of improvement. I stayed stoic and solemn, a soldier to the end.

In the end, I was diagnosed with various mood disorders and a couple of psychoses with names I can't pronounce.

"Do you even realize you're not thinking clearly?" someone asked me.

My thoughts were spinning around in beautiful synchronicity. "They make sense to me. You're just not listening properly."

The resident, patient philosopher, a curmudgeonly, avuncular looking seventy-plus type, after he saw my exasperated expression from several days of psychiatric grilling by three bespectacled, pencil-necked Staff Psychiatrists said, "For now, we see through a glass darkly....and all that." Whatever that means? He explained what he meant to me several times—but I apparently didn't get it.

At the end of this marathon mind mending, the chief psychiatrist, a very affable Scotsman, announced that he was going to Mexico for an extended holiday. I'm not sure whether this was preplanned or if having me as a patient for four days did him in, but I haven't seen him since.

Starting the very evening of my diagnoses day, Nurse Ratched, this time with the distinct facial expression of a garden gnome, arrived to meet me holding a tray with a cocktail of many-colored, variable shaped, medications, supposedly designed to settle me down.

"You've been prescribed a heavy regimen of medication to control your unruly urges and intolerant thoughts," she explained. I shivered as, through the fog, I remembered McMurphy's smothering fate.

I tried to palm the pills to throw them away later, but she was too vigilant to be fooled by an incalcitrant patient. Her many years of experience in psychiatric and rehabilitation units had taught her to trust no one. Or maybe she was just mean—she had plenty of practice at that too.

"You can take them on your own, or the orderlies will come to help," she declared. "Or I can call your wife."

I took the damn pills.

That night, I slept. I slept all night, not waking up once, until my bladder's demand in the morning.

I could feel my thoughts slowing. I could see that beautiful synchronicity of brilliance fading away. But I knew there was no choice. Either I took the pills or I'd have them forced down me. Perhaps not by the orderlies, but certainly by my wife.

I think I would have preferred the orderlies. But I took the pills.

After the third day on the elixir, I woke up to clear vision. I couldn't see my thoughts anymore. Nothing shimmered. Nothing reshaped itself to be better or more efficient. All I could see was... my actual surroundings.

I felt... bare.

But, as Churchill said, if you're walking through hell, it's best to keep walking. Maybe I was in hell. Maybe I wasn't. But I needed to keep walking, because that's the only way to get anywhere.

So I... surrendered.

I decided to take the advice of the experts. Maybe Nurse Ratched was mean, but she also had decades of experience. I got to know the group. There was a giant guy whose name was Elmer. He was friendly enough, but every occasionally, he got a look on his face like he wanted to cut one of us reckless, unruly, recalcitrants. Since they wouldn't let him have a knife or a hatchet, I thought he would probably resort to smothering anyone who crossed him. I gave Elmer a wide berth and kept uncharacteristically quiet whenever he was around. Was I destined to the same unceremonious smothering as Randall McMurphy?

In this surreal state, I finally submitted to the inevitable. The defensive ramparts I had carefully constructed over a lifetime of alcohol excess were battered down.

Once I was willing to listen, my counselors and peers gave me great steaming shovels full of "feedback" daily. Feedback is a codeword for honest assessment, (often brutally honest assessment) of both negative and positive behaviors, traits etc., observed during the treatment process. In time, a symbiotic relationship evolves between peers who give and take feedback. A strange phenomenon develops where the person making the assessment profits equally, or more so, with the person on the receiving end. A sympathetic, compassionate bond occurs that cannot be explained in this short space. I believe it had a lot to do with shared suffering and the camaraderie that develops between hurting kindred spirits. Suffice it to say that it works. Alcoholics become sober, addicts become clean, and the mentally ill become... less so.

And then, one day in therapy, I realized that I was laughing.

I am now a believer. Maplewood has a tried and tested methodology, and despite the determination of a continuing crew of 'Arrogant Controlling Perfectionists in Defiant Denial,' like me, trying to sabotage the operation—it works.

Maplewood took me on in mid Feb 07. I arrived full of anger, fear, and mistrust. With the help of my peers and counselors, I left with a curious mixture of hope, peace, and anxiety. After fifty-two days, I joined the ranks of the millions of happy recovering alcoholics embracing the Alcoholics Anonymous Fellowship.

I've waited in a lot of line-ups in my seven decades, but this one was to offer the most valuable and enduring reward. Maplewood has given me a new lease on life. It was worth it to wait patiently.

And I laugh quite often now.

YOGA

I had been feeling tired for a while. I was pale and listless, with bluish-coloured lips and fingernails. After I had lost more than fifty pounds, my brother Jake said, confidentially, of course, that I "looked like a cadaverous, skeletal Smurf."

My cardiologist got all the test reports back. "I'm afraid I have some disturbing news Mr. Webb," he said in a solemn voice. "You are very ill." It was bad news by anybody's estimation. I was going to die shortly; he gave me six months, max.

According to the medical assessment, I had dilated cardio monopoly—or something like that. In layman's terms, the doc told me, my heart was pumping at 23%; the minimum rate for healthy people was 55%. Also, he went on to report, I suffered from atrial fibrillation (irregular heartbeat) and hypoxemia (lack of oxygen—that was what caused the blue lips). It was mostly from drinking and smoking too much during my 40-plus years in the Army. I was a wreck.

I could imagine the Grim Reaper standing menacingly at the door, dressed in his black hoodie and holding a sickle in his bony hands, taking me off to my fate in heaven, or hell, whichever my lifetime Big Book diary in the sky permitted.

He looked me in the eye. He was a gnome-like creature of about 4 feet 10, so he had to look up; and grimly read from the chart in front of him. The bottom line was that without emergency intervention (his words) I was subject to sudden death from massive cardio infarction (heart attack) or stroke. He gave it another term, but I can't spell it, or pronounce it for that matter.

After consultation with a couple of his colleagues in the heart business, he gave me his prognosis and a treatment plan for a cardio version (shock to the heart to regain normal rhythm), a half dozen medications, a referral to a respirologist (oxygen guy) and a possibility of an implanted cardiac defibrillator (pace maker type contraption; another gizmo that keeps the heart ticking— my words). He also mentioned another gizmo that would shock the heart immediately back to life if it stopped. The doc said that "it was like the frying pans you see being used on TV by emergency medical staff to revive dead people." Trying to make me relax, he explained, "it would be implanted in my chest, so I wouldn't forget it or forget to turn it on." This was not terribly comforting, but I nodded my head up and down to confirm a vague understanding.

I got my affairs in order by making up what I called the 'Dead Book' for my wife, telling her where all my money was hidden, what stuff I wanted to give away and to whom, and preparing a power of attorney in case I didn't die and became a vegetable instead, and she had to pull the plug. "When somebody has to wipe my butt, shoot me," I confided in her.

That reminds me, I must get that power of attorney cancelled; she's a pretty good shot.

We quickly made up a bucket list of three or four trips I wanted to make before I croaked. We did two of the trips, to Alaska and the East Coast in the first three months, when I got the word from the heart clinic that my heart extraction was at 34% I might not snuff after all. With great relief, I told my friends and relatives the news. My brother Jake asked me if he had to give back my shotgun and fishing tackle that I'd given him when I thought my hunting and fishing days were over. My wife was ecstatic, the doctor was stunned; I think he lost the bet with his fellow cardiologists that I was done for. He recommended that I do more exercise and to lose my beer belly (the twins he called it). He also made me up a diet of 'rabbit food' mostly fruit and veggies chicken and fish that I should eat from now on made up of all the stuff that I hated like broccoli, carrots and cabbage.

"You mean I can't have pizza, beer and butter tarts anymore," I lamented. The doctor looked at me derisively and gestured toward the door.

I thought of running or even jogging but that's too hard (I noticed that nobody that I saw jogging had a smile on their face). Swimming was out—I got water-logged whenever I swam and sunk to the bottom. Didn't like water. Tennis had too many balls, bowling didn't have enough. Baseball was out—I didn't chew tobacco and tried not to scratch my crotch in public. I was too small and short for basketball and too big and tall to jockey. Golf didn't interest me—it always reminded me of a quote by George Bernard Shaw that "golf is a good walk ruined." That left lawn bowling, something called Ty Cheese and Yogi. My wife quickly corrected me saying "it's 'yoga' stoop, not Yogi; that's Yogi bear you're thinking of. "Oh yeah,' I said, Yogi and Boo Boo; will I see them there?" I thought for a minute, then blurted, "And do they serve cheese in Ty cheese?" She was not impressed at my attempt at levity. Maybe she didn't get it.

I chose yoga because the name was shorter, and I could spell it and it sounded a lot like yogurt which I liked—the sweet stuff that is. Besides, Ty cheese and lawn bowling were for old people. And I was only 70.

I read up on the history of yoga and found out that yoga was developed in India 5000 years ago and there were 200,000 practitioners worldwide. Also, I found out that Robert Downey junior was one of them. "Good enough for Iron Man, it's good enough for me," I mumbled to nobody in particular. Wikipedia told me that "yoga is a group of physical, mental and spiritual practices or disciplines originated in ancient India." It went on to say that, "There is a broad variety of yoga moves and goals in Hinduism. Buddhism and Jainism," and a couple of other 'isms' The gurus related to Yoga were a were people with unpronounceable names like Iyenger, Knshnamahaya and Swami Vivekananda.

Then I asked a couple of my Army buddies what they thought about yoga to get the real story:

"I do yoga so I can be flexible enough to kick my own arse when necessary" one old tanker said with a glint in his eye. (He only had one eye). Another old gunner smirked and said, "I heard the motto of yoga is 'Don't just do something, sit there." That's good enough for me, I thought. "Do you have to sweat," I asked as an afterthought.

"Not unless it's real hot and you have a Drill Sergeant as a yogi" my buddy opined. "All right then, Yoga it is." I said to myself.

I enquired at the Kingston Seniors about yoga classes, "what are the prerequisites? I asked of a willowy octogenarian volunteer sitting at the information desk. I also inquired if there were "any drill sergeants on staff."

There was a pause, as she considered my question: "well I guess a pulse and no obvious missing limbs, and we don't have any drill sergeants" the volunteer quoted. (I think she made that up). Anyway, I was relieved when she told me "the lowest level course is designed to be painless with no sweating and minimum movement. You could even do it while sitting down in a chair. "I'm in!"

"Will it help your oxygen? Does it help with ED?" I whispered conspiratorially to the cadaverous-looking male volunteer at the adjoining wicket. Not sure why. Guess I thought he could use a laugh to get his heart going. He suddenly appeared to wake up and squeaked "I think so; never needed it myself."

"That sounds good," I said. "Sign me up."

I had a bit of trouble getting the right outfit to wear. They said they didn't have a size 50 singlet or size 44 yoga tights at the yoga store. On recommendation from the yoga people my next stop was at the ballet shop, across town. I asked about the tights that the men wore, "You know, the ones with the orange in the crotch, like Baryshnikov wears. "A scrawny scare-crow of a sales lady with pince-nez glasses, and a bun on the back of her head grabbed me by the arm and escorted me out. No sense of humour, these people.

I had a bit better luck at a sports apparel store where the clerk advised "Why don't you check out the wrestling equipment shop across the bridge on the left?" I did and bought the biggest set of wrestling tights they had. They were black at least; I couldn't see myself in the pink or powder-blue. But, they weren't big enough, it turned out.

Well, I finally made it to my first and as it turned out, my last yoga class. Clad in my new wrestling tights, which restricted my breathing and circulation somewhat, a trifle tight, I showed up slightly late. The instructor asked, "are you Bill?" I nodded. 'Well come up here to the front" she continued with a broad grin. She put me at the front of the class, in the only vacant spot which everyone else had avoided. I quickly spread out my mat and pillow and awaited the words of command from the yogi with bated breath.

After she explained that in ancient times, the desire for greater personal freedom, health, long life and self-understanding gave birth to this system of physical and mental exercises. Our focus would be on balance, strength and the muscles involved would all of them except maybe the ears.

Then, she told everyone to take off their shoes and socks. (Barefoot for yoga, you see). I looked around at an assortment of alien lower appendages. They were, well, all gnarly, with bunions and corns and calluses, and hammer toes as big as your thumb. So, we started the class with a couple of "Homm, Homms." Then we went through a number of basic yoga poses with, again, unpronounceable names. In English, they were named after animals such as frogs, cows, swans and inanimate objects such as trees, and even insects – locusts. The warrior pose was my favourite, until I was forced to do it. 'Pain.'

Finally, we got down to the 'Down Dirty Dog,' as I called it, a stretching movement where you start on your hands and knees and then elevate your butt as high as you can, stretching out both arms and legs. Not a pretty sight; especially when your tights are too tight.

The Yogi said this was to stretch some strange sounding muscle that I had never heard of. After I asked her what it was in simple soldier terms, three times, she blurted out "it's between your scrotum and your anus!"

"Oh, the taint, I said. 'taint your bag and taint your arse?" She covered her ears and sighed as one of the ladies from immediately behind me, fearful-looking, and fidgeting, went up and whispered something in her ear.

"Bill," the Yogi said, a little exasperated "can you move to the back of the class?" She told me later that I was scaring the ladies behind me doing the down dirty dog. Apparently, my junk was bulging out which didn't leave too much to the imagination—especially with those immediately behind me. "Guess they haven't seen a real man before," I said. With that, she unceremoniously escorted me to the front desk where the willowy woman and cadaverous man were sitting and told them to "refund my money, since yoga was not a good fit for me?" It was either me or the sixteen little old ladies in the class. Simple economic concerns prevailed. I was out.

My first and last (I was asked not to return) yoga class was not a success. I would have to find another form of exercise. Glumly, (well not too glumly) I went to the Dairy Queen to treat myself to a chocolate sundae. It might make me feel better, I thought.

I was stiff from moving parts that I'd never moved before and my arthritic knee and ankle (old soldier injuries) were acting up. Limping gingerly up to the counter at the Dairy Queen, I ordered my sundae. After about a minute, a giant scrumptious sundae, dripping with chocolate and smothered in maraschino cherries, appeared. This was going to be good.

"Crushed nuts?" asked the smiling girl behind the counter.

"No," I said. "Yoga."

GI

Medical science has become a juggernaut. From the achingly slow progress of taking centuries to realize that cleanliness was helpful and bloodletting was not to the discovery of opium as painkiller, vaccines, x-rays, radiation poisoning, opioid addiction, and now the inevitable rush toward genetic editing and cloning and 3-d printing to create new internal organs, it feels like we'll soon be capable of miracles. The reach of technology and the scope of humanity's imagination is without limit.

As someone who is no longer young, I'm rather grateful for this phenomena. The inevitability of aging is something we all must come to terms with, seeing our bodies deteriorate and give in to the pains, embarrassments, and inconveniences we once pitied in our parents and grandparents.

That embarrassment solidified for me when I realized that I was having abdominal discomfort of the lower tract, gastrointestinal disturbances of a severe nature. I was experiencing intense bloating accompanied by unpredictable and premature emissions. My condition was the butt of seventy-three percent of adolescent male jokes, the reality that we try to hide from our significant others early in the courtship, the inevitable human condition everyone experiences (to some degree) and nobody wants to talk about.

Yes, I had gas. Loud, painful, explosive, unromantic, odiferous gas. If we're going to be medically formal about it, I was experiencing flatulence.

If we're going to be blunt, I was farting, a lot, at inconvenient times, in inconvenient places, and no amount of clenching my rear admiral could stop it.

To the uninitiated and apathetic observer, (and every nine-year-old male) this condition was nothing less than hilarious. However, to the veteran sufferer it was not at all funny; the pain could be excruciating, to say nothing of the embarrassment.

I tried several home remedies and sure-fire pharmacological fixes recommended by my fellow afflicted. These included cranberry juice in two daily doses administered at dawn and dusk. I also did toe touches and deep knee bends (to push out the offending vapours) as recommended by a fitness freak friend of mine. A (very) amateur dietician told me to eat a half a pound of old cheddar cheese a day, supposedly to keep the vapours in. Other prescriptions included drinking gallons of Diovol and gobbling down six packs of Tums and bottled water laced with liberal applications of bicarbonate of soda and ENO fruit salts. I even, on advice from a great uncle, took hot toddies of cider-vinegar and honey with a pinch of nutmeg for a while. None of these cures offered more than temporary relief, and in the case of hot toddies the medicine turned out to be worse than the disease. It might have been the rum I added to the mix. I had to kill that vinegar taste with something. Rum worked well, but I think it detracted somewhat from the effectiveness of the elixir.

Even restricting my diet to the blandest of meals, including fruits veggies, seaweed, and tofu (no more of my favourite beer and pizza) did not provide relief. After turning orange from eating too many carrots, I took another track.

I was forced, through bitter sometimes hilarious trial and error, at last, to seek the professional help of the medical branch. The doctors, nurses, and other highly skilled clinicians put me through the normal regimen of physiological tests, including blood samples, x-rays, and urine tests. Finally, I was referred to who was considered the best belly doctor in the Region. He was a small man with delicate features, and he seemed always to be late like the rabbit in *Alice in Wonderland*. He asked me a battery of questions, which traced my genealogy and medical history back to Noah's ark. Next, he wanted to know everything I'd eaten or drank for the past forty years. He was very thorough, to say the least, and obviously a most competent practitioner of medical science in the gastrointestinal field.

Unfortunately, his probing was inconclusive and I would have to travel to a higher qualified specialist for more definitive testing at a larger hospital. This was arranged, and after a couple of months on the waiting list, I found myself sitting on a bench in a skimpy light blue gown (with the back cut out of it, obviously designed for easy access). It was starched so thoroughly that it would probably stand up by itself. A couple of gowns thrown on the top of the laundry pile in the corner looked like they were facing off at hockey game. In front of a door marked 'GI Lab,' several other unfortunates who sat beside me, similarly clad and with quizzical vacant stares on their faces, did nothing to improve my discomfiture.

Finally, after an hour or so of crossing and uncrossing my legs and watching my fellow victims disappear into the maw of the "GI Lab", never to return. It was my turn.

As I entered the room, I was surrounded by towering stainless-steel machines that seemed to blink and whirr in unison to greet me. A white-frocked technician, garlanded with a couple of stethoscopes, and at least a dozen pens in a case in the breast pocket methodically and professionally strapped me into a gyro-type apparatus not unlike an astronaut's seat console. He then gave me detailed instructions on when to breathe and when to swallow a thick chalky, milk-shake-like liquid; above all, he told me not to be nervous or concerned as the machine turned me upside down and shook me sideways like a ride at the country fair. He'd been "in the gastro business for five years running these machines," he said, and "hadn't lost a patient yet." (I was convinced that I was destined to be the first casualty, most likely a fatality). I could see the headlines in the local paper, "Man flies off the Gyro machine at Memorial Hospital and is thrown out the window on the eighth floor. His gas has been cured."

After my twenty-minute ride on the 'Gyro' was over, I was sent to the ultrasound department, suffering slightly from vertigo but otherwise no worse for wear. Here, I was covered with a greasy, slimy, purple-coloured liquid and then methodically poked for a half hour or so with a metallic probe which according to the operator worked something like sonar on a submarine to survey the GI system. As the probe was passed over my stomach, a television console display showed wavy lines and shaded patterns of my organs which apparently made sense to someone, not me. It was all very scientific and in a word, Greek, to me.

After several other minor tests (less memorable, at least), I was allowed to get out of my backless light blue gown and await the verdict from the experts. A very business-like doctor (without the white frock) and with several testing devices, which resembled large fountain pens, protruding from his pockets, approached me officiously with an arm full of computer print outs hanging down to the floor. I thought he was in danger of tripping.

He pointed out all the squiggly lines and funny shaded images, with each accompanied by a patter of medical terminology that only highly trained GI specialists could possibly understand.

After about ten minutes of this technical talk, and after my eyes glazed over, he realized that I didn't have the foggiest idea of what he was saying. He then reluctantly reverted to laymen's language.

"The tests we have given you," he commented, "are the best available at any medical facility in Canada. "We think we've discovered your problem."

Well, that was good news. Knowing the problem is a good step toward actually solving it.

"Sir," he continued, in a triumphant almost conspiratorial tone "You've got GAS."

Great Expectations

Saint Valentine's Day has evolved into a colossal commercial enterprise eclipsed only by Christmas. The dictionary defines Saint Valentine's Day as a day when valentines, that is, greeting cards or tokens of affection, are exchanged with sweethearts. Some say it is the yearly opportunity for men to apologize for all their misdemeanors, misbehavior and lack of romantic attention to their partners for the previous year; to ease their guilt and placate their beloveds. Regardless, of the root cause of this phenomenon, beaux go batty for at least one day a year.

In recent times, the tokens have grown in grandeur, and everything, from chocolate hearts to new cars and Caribbean cruises, is sold to lovesick suitors. Harried husbands strive to outdo each other by spending more money or showing more imagination than their peers. They lavish their sweethearts with flowers (the florist business booms with blooms) and gift certificates for everything from exclusive spa visits to oil changes. I would not recommend oil changes as a Valentine gift. My brother Steve tried it when they had a special at Midas Muffler, reasoning that he was saving money for his new snowmobile and didn't need to buy an elaborate gift.

Instead of a new snowmobile, he ended up buying a diamond necklace, and he's finally allowed back into the bedroom.

The Valentine's Day celebration probably developed from its coincidental falling so close to Lupercalia, an ancient fertility festival held on 15 February. The feast was celebrated in Rome, in honor of the rustic, licentious, deity Lupercus. Ancient mythology also claims that the spirits of passion roam the earth on Valentine's Day, scattering their elixirs among vulnerable, unsuspecting mortals. Spouses and beaus are enticed by Eros and charmed by Cupid. Ethereal romantic energy stalks the earth (unless a spouse decides that an oil change is a nice gift).

A few years ago, quite a few years ago actually, in the late eighties, I was rudely reminded of the crass commercialism of our modern Valentine's Day. It was a week before, V-day, when I decided to buy my wife a nice pair of earrings. Being frugal, I reviewed several copies of the Whig, the local newspaper, and got out as many flyers as I could find to look for sales. Several of the stores in town offered jewelry at reduced prices, some up to 50% off, and two stores had specials on earrings. The closest one to where I worked, at Fort Frontenac, was on the lower half of Princess Street. I would venture over there as soon as I could, before they were all scooped up by the roaming love-sick suitors in the city with limited funds. My plan was falling together.

On that day, because of a formal retirement luncheon for an old comrade at work, I wore my best (my only) three-piece grey pinstripe suit with my brown Dacks wing-tip shoes. It sported the stylish contemporary accoutrements of the time, a medium-width purple tie with an almost matching mauve handkerchief in the left breast pocket. Even if I do say so myself, I looked rather dapper, "like a natty white-collared Bay Street Banker," one of my colleagues commented.

Valentine's Day that year was unseasonably warm, and townsfolk promenaded along Princess Street, soaking up the solar rays of a tantalizing sun. Softening ice crunched under my wing tips as I walked, with a spring in my step, toward the jewelry store. Rivulets of melt water swished down the gutters. It was glorious weather for the time of year. I was determined to get there before the crowd of last-minute men descended on the place, like locusts, in an attempt to get the best deals. My expectations for this day were great.

I entered the store and started browsing in the earring section right away. Several other husbands were in the store, obviously, like me, looking for bargains before they could be snatched up by the multitude of milling men. A large, bewhiskered man in a checkered flannel shirt, denim jeans and steel-toed work boots was fondling a necklace which looked like a trinket in his huge meaty paw. Leaving him, abruptly, at the necklace counter, an excessively made-up clerk with a glued-on smile rushed over to meet me with undue haste. She reminded me of Dickens's Miss Havisham, an eccentric recluse. She lived in a gloomy locked mansion, where all clocks had been stopped on the day that her betrothed bridegroom had jilted her. The wedding meal moldered in a dark, dank, and dusty, unused dining room. Habitually, she dressed in her wedding dress, tattered and yellowed with age. She was the virtual virgin of vindictiveness.

Hopefully this particular Miss Havisham was not so bad and would assist me in my quest for a moderately inexpensive, but high quality, exquisite, pair of earrings. Not too inexpensive though; that would be gauche, my wife would think I cheap (which I guess I was), but she would not be impressed. I was reminded of a fellow officer who bought his wife a frying pan for Christmas. "The old one is kind of beat up" he said, with a feigned look of concern on his face. "She'll be happy that I noticed," he said as an afterthought.

She still reminds him of this faux pas at every opportunity. He was a good example to his fellows of what not to do.

Now to resume the tale of my Miss Havisham at the jewelry store: After the requisite, "How may I help you?" and before I had a chance to inquire about their specials, she whisked me down to the end of the counter where a small ornate oak cabinet with clouded blue tinted glass awaited in a remote corner of the store. With an antique-looking gold key, which hung around her neck on a thick silver cord, she carefully opened it. She then proceeded to show me an impressive selection of glittering earrings. She went on with the obnoxious, condescending patter of a used car salesman informing me in detail of the origin of each specific piece.

After a quick inspection, I noticed a particularly fine-looking pair that I was sure my wife would like, and asked the obvious question, "How much?"

"They are Eight-nine-ninety-five," she said in a too soft conspiratorial voice. I asked her to repeat it and she said it again one decibel louder. "Eight-nine-ninety-five" she recited. I hadn't really heard her clearly, with my hearing loss from over twenty years in the Army, but in embarrassment, I nodded my approval.

As I was contemplating the purchase, she expectantly rummaged under the counter, and produced an elegant gold embossed box, with the store logo, a caricature of a lion, on top, and vellum-like, pink paisley wrapping paper. "I'll take them," I said, and casually handed her a crisp $100.00 bill with a feigned flourish.

Before my eyes, there was a total metamorphosis: the colour drained from the clerk's already waxy-white colored face. Her starched smile turned to the derisive smirk of Cruella De Ville. She was what some people called gob-smacked.

Finally, she recovered, lifted an eyebrow, pursed her lips in distaste and said, "That's eight-hundred and ninety-five-dollars" (Big bucks in those days). She articulated this in a practiced monotone, and emphasized each word—loudly, so all in the store, and I'm sure some outside, could hear.

"Could we move to the left a couple of decimal points?" I stammered, trying to remain nonchalant—with limited success.

The clerk did not reply; she was struck mute. Suddenly the fawning attention ceased. She gave me the evil eye, for what seemed an eternity, and then abandoned me dismissively, to attend to more deserving victims— with fatter wallets.

Attempting to recover some of my ruffled dignity, I straightened myself up to my full height and puffed out my chest with the purple hanky. Performing a quick left turn, I marched down the store's length to the door. Miss Havisham's penetrating glare drilled into the back of my head all the way out. Chastened, I left the store and headed for the comfort of the mall, where kinder, gentler, sales clerks abound. One of said clerks did help me find a lovely silver chain with a rose quartz pendant for, ironically, eighty-nine dollars and change.

I still get shaky when Valentine's Day approaches— or when I get within sight of that jewelry store.

That woman was an absolute Dickensian... and my great expectations have been marred forever.

NORTHERN ODYSSEY

I was approaching seventy and not in great health after over forty years' service in the Army and too much rough and riotous living. I was having trouble walking and experienced some shortness of breath. So I had to ask the doctor what the hell was wrong with me.

He looked me in the eye. "Two things. You're old and you're fat; you can't do anything about being old, but you can lose weight if you live healthy."

Virgil, the ancient Roman poet wrote "The greatest wealth is health." I think he made that up.

The doctor diagnosed me with heart disease, nocturnal hypoxemia (weak lungs at night), osteo-arthritis and a few other old-age ailments. A respirologist specialist outfitted me with a contraption called a BPAP to help with breathing at night, and my GP gave me prescriptions for massage, acupuncture, and orthotics, along with a cocktail of medications.

"Seventy isn't so old" I thought; after all it's only twenty-one in Celsius, 10 in dog years. Unfortunately, I was neither thermometer nor dog. My maternal great-grandmother often said that she was as "old as the itch." I'm not sure what she meant, or where she got that from, or what itch she was talking about, but she lived into her late nineties. Not to be outdone, my paternal great-grandmother also a nonagenarian, often jested that "growing old was not for sissies," and then she quickly added "but the alternative is quite discouraging." Often when she said that, she had a cigarette in her hand and a glass of sherry in front of her. "Smoking and drinking are good for your health," she would recite. "Look at Churchill, and what about George Burns. They smoked cigars; I don't smoke cigars."

I did a bit of research on sixty-five-plus citizens in my local area. According to Vital Signs 2017, a Community Foundation for Kingston and Area, "Seniors have outnumbered children in Kingston since 2008." Put simply, "In 2016, 2 of 10 residents in the Kingston census were sixty-five-plus." By 2026, 3 of 10 are projected to be over sixty-five. We were gaining on the kids. Whether this turns out to be good or bad remains to be seen—daycare for seniors, anyone?

There are of course some advantages to be a senior citizen. You get a lot of senior's discounts at stores like Shopper's Drug Mart, Denny's, and the Salvation Army, to name a few. Being frugal (some would say cheap) I went to the Sally Ann for my post-weight-loss summer wardrobe when there was a 50% discount for seniors. I bought about fifty bucks worth of clothing; I think I got eight T-shirts, four pairs of shorts, two pairs of pants, two sweaters, a jacket, five DVDs and a scarf for my wife. When I went up to the cash to pay, I saw more discounts advertised; 25% student discount, 25% military discount and 10% blue tag sale. I'm a student, I thought; I took a safe driving course at the Kingston Seniors last year, I'm also a veteran, military/veteran, close enough, I surmised. I don't know what blue tag is, but I'll take it. This is amazing, I thought. What a country this is. Who else would give you 110% discount, senior or not?

After a bit of quick calculating in my head, I said to the lady behind the cash, "You guys owe me ten bucks." She called the manager, a large hairy man (I think). If this manager was a woman, she had a nice moustache and forearms like Popeye. They showed me the door; I did not argue. They had a steely-look that chilled even a seasoned veteran such as myself.

No sense of humour these Salvation Army people.

They say that seventy is the new sixty; but, a fellow veteran of mine in his nineties reminded me that the new dead is now sick unless you look after your health. He also mentioned philosophically, that "we all start out in diapers and would all end up in diapers." And just to be thorough, he mentioned that "you were getting old when you forgot to pull your zipper up; but you were even older when you forgot to pull it down?"

Sitting in his walker, he lamented the adage, that "If I knew I was going to live this long, I would have taken better care of myself."

Amen to that.

So, I decided to listen to my doctor (for once) and lose weight, eat healthy, and get more active, the trending triumvirate of good health for seniors (and anybody else, for that matter). I was referred to a dietician, apparently, good health is impossible without good nutrition. She coached me in balanced diets, portion size and timings for dining. My next stop was at the dog breeders to get a small but active dog with a good temperament. The good temperament was essential, because my normal temperament was well, bad. To be honest, I really didn't like people. The dog could counter act my frequent sour moods, I thought. Or, with luck, my bad moods might even improve with social interaction.

We bought a popular active and calm mixed breed, which took care of the active (and good-natured) requirement. In six short months, I lost forty pounds walking Finnegan, our new Australian mini Labradoodle. I've begun to suspect he has some kangaroo blood too; he has huge, powerful, back legs and jumps up over six feet from a standing start to get a treat.

We strolled twice a day for two or three clicks. I won't say I had a six-pack after several months of this, but my case of twenty-four was starting to shrink. I had to lose the twins, as my doctor ordered. I think I had triplets when I started.

I felt good; I had energy for the first time in years, slept well, and even looked better in my clothes. Pants and shirts that I hadn't worn for years now fit comfortably. I decided that I was ready to go out in public again. I even started to get a better outlook on life, and started to tolerate people, started to shed my moroseness. I still couldn't smile much though; it hurt my face. Lack of use, I guess.

For a long time, Alaska had been on my bucket list. Several trips while serving in the Army just showed me what an Arctic Base looked like and what the flat expanse of tundra looks like from a helicopter, or from a parachute. I read all the pamphlets and brochures I could find, and my wife booked our tickets; (I don't have the patience to wait on the phone anymore; witnessed by the smashed phones in the door by the sink).

I was intrigued with the motivation of the people who would live in the Arctic, north of 60, by choice and why it was mostly adventurers, seeking their fortune, those running away from something, and those who weren't sure why they were there – or where they were going. Students made up most of the itinerant workers which doubled the population in tourist season.

So we decided along with my brother and his wife, to take the combined cruise and overland voyage to Alaska, Northern British Columbia, and the Yukon Territory. We sailed on the cruise liner Holland America from Vancouver, the crown jewel of Western Canada, through the inside passage, hugging the west coast, between the islands of British Columbia and Alaska from Vancouver to Juneau, Alaska. On the ship, we saw the misty fjords of the coast, and the blue turquoise glaciers thundering as they retreat to reveal new-born land. Small icebergs (growlers), and not so small icebergs, floated by on most days. We sailed past Prince Rupert B.C., a major shipping port, home of a magnificent fourteen-mile long harbour, and one of the deepest, natural, ice-free harbours in the world, serving the Asia-Pacific trade corridor as a transportation hub. A tall Texan, wearing a black cowboy hat, bragged that they had bigger, longer, more modern harbours on the Gulf Coast. "But, do you have grizzly bears and polar bears?" a local Alaskan asked.

"No, but we have oil refineries where we turn Alaska crude into gas and diesel," the Texan shot back.

I've seen oil refineries; I'd rather deal with the bears.

Next, we sailed past Ketchikan, Alaska's first established city, a community of 14,000. with the largest collection of totem poles in the world. At the turn of the century, Ketchikan flourished in the fishing industry, and later, mining and timber operations developed. It became an important trading community. And as an aside, like many of the burgeoning gold-rush towns, an estimated two thirds of the miner's wages reportedly ended up in the bars, gambling houses, and bordellos of the downtown red light district, Creek Street. Things really don't change that much; Creek Street just migrated to Nevada and became Las Vegas.

Sitka was the next community of note that we sailed past. Sitka, with a population of 9000, was the seat of the Russian Empire in North America from the 1700s until Alaska was purchased by the United States in 1867. It remained the Alaskan capital until 1912. Again, the guy from Texas, not to be outdone, said "Those Ruskies are kicking their butts now. They sold us Alaska for something like seven million dollars. That's about one minute of oil flowing through the four–foot pipeline from Prudhoe Bay to Valdez, 24/7. We got them on that one."

Our first port of call was Juneau, again in Alaska, and the current capital with a population of 32,000. Also founded by the gold miners of the Great Gold Rush of the late 1800s and early 1900s. Juneau has a rich history, apparently, but I didn't hear much about it. It was time for my daily nap, so I missed our first port of call. We had seen a movie about King Arthur and the Round Table not long before; so, my wife and brother started calling me "Sir-naps-a-lot." I made no apologies; I was just obeying my doctor.

He told me to get plenty of rest.

Our next stop was Scagway, the northernmost point in Alaska's inside passage. There was a steady drizzle falling as we walked down the gangplank and into the town. The locals called it "liquid sunshine." In its heyday, Scagway was the boomtown gateway to the Trail of 98 and the Klondike Gold Fields. Scagway was also the first incorporated city in Alaska on June 28, 1900.

Scagway has a population of over 1200 hardy permanent citizens during the winter off-season, but when the summer tourist season arrives, the population swells to over 2500 mostly from the lower 48. Scagway is advertised in the local paper, Scagway Alaskan, as "The Premiere Shopping and Dining Experience" in Alaska.

Several unique attractions were listed including: the Klondike Doughboy, which featured Alaskan fry bread and reindeer sausage. The Brothel Museum daily tours were advertised as

$10.00 for twenty minutes at the Red Onion Saloon; twenty minutes of what, it didn't say. Apparently this was the same price the miners paid a century ago, though I'm certain that wasn't simply for a tour of the brothel. "Where the ladies never miss a trick," another sign said, in small print. I asked my wife if they were magicians or jugglers or something?

Also, hot baths were advertised for 10 cents; group rates were also available. (Rub-a-dub dub, three men in the tub; or two men and one woman or perhaps two women and one lucky man). The combination is limited only by one's imagination.

One guide told us that Scagway had over sixty jewellery and souvenir shops and that it was the law in Alaska for tourists not to be more than fifty feet from a gift store at any one time. I don't think we ever were, except when we were flying, perhaps.

Another claim to fame has put Scagway in the Guinness World Record Book for the most people ever assembled for an egg toss. On 1July, 2008, Scagway shattered the Previous Guinness record by assembling 1,162 egg tossers—half the local population. The line stretched for four blocks on the main Broadway street; that must have been one huge omelet. It was 'eggsactly' what they'd planned.

Scagway was at the centre of the 1897 Gold Rush. Gold was discovered in mid August 1896 in the Klondike, Yukon Territory. When word of the discovery reached the outside world in 1897, it sparked an unprecedented stampede. An estimated 100,000 would-be prospectors left home in the lower 48 for the gold fields. Even over a century later the words 'Chilcot' and 'Klondike' bring back images of the North, adventure, hardship, and gold. Most of the adventurers returned broken financially, physically, and spiritually. One anonymous wag was recorded as lamenting that "[i]t was a sourdough experience; when things went sour, and the dough ran out, we had enough experience and went home." I don't blame them a bit.

Poems, short stories and novels from the time forged the reputations of writers like Robert Service, Jack London, and Pierre Berton. Service, The Canadian 'Yukon Poet' wrote the famous, often quoted *Cremation of Sam McGee* (There are strange thing done in the midnight sun by the men who moil for gold) and *the Shooting of Dan Mc Grew* (Some of the boys were whooping it up in the Malamute Saloon).

Jack London, the celebrated American author, wrote the renown novels *Call of the Wild* and *White Fang*, now widely read as classics.

Pierre Berton, born in Whitehorse, wrote mostly non-fiction like the *Klondike* along with dozens of other works including his excellent *Vimy.*

In 1896, the discovery was made on Rabbit Creek, a small tributary to the Klondike River, which was later named Bonanza River. A few became fabulously wealthy, taking millions of dollars in today's money from the creeks. When the first wave of these successful stampeders returned to the lower 48, the great gold rush began in earnest when the headline of the *Intelligencer* in Seattle described the mother lode discovered in the north. By 1898, Scagway was the largest city in Alaska.

Entrepreneurs and all manner of con men descended on the unsuspecting stampeders. Immediately after the tens of thousands of gold rushers arrived, searching for pay dirt (gold dust). As any place of that era where the young men were numerous, the money was abundant, and the women scarce, the muddy streets of Scagway were inundated with saloons, gambling houses, and brothels.

Here, we learned about the villain of Scagway, named Soapy Smith and his gang, who cheated the gold rushers out of their gold, in their typical sin palaces. They mined the miners, so to speak.

He and his mafia-like associates made up of con men and thieves, and even murderers, swindled prospectors with cards, dice, shell games, and prostitution. Soapy Smith ruled the town. He even controlled a private militia called the Saguay Military Company, the town newspaper and the Deputy U.S. Marshall who he kept in his pay with bribes and intimidation. Soapy was the Al Capone of Scagway.

Soapy also ran a telegraph service for messages coming in and going out to destinations all over the world for $5.00 a shot. It was discovered after Soapy's unfortunate demise from being shot dead (by a town father) that the telegraph wire was tied to a tree a couple mile outside of Scagway. People finally understood why their telegrams were going unanswered.

He and his gang also initiated what became known as a soap scheme. They would sell soap for a dollar a bar, quite a sum in those days, with a chance to win a fifty-dollar bill advertised to be hidden in one bar in each box of 50 bars.

The fifty-dollar bill, however, was slipped surreptitiously to one of their accessories to the crime, who stood in line with the unsuspecting public. Quite ingenious, this was worthy of Houdini. Old Soapy was slippery.

We were entertained by "The Days of 98 Show," Alaska's longest running musical, first presented in 1923. It was advertised as a tuneful tale of good old Soapy Smith. The show included Robert Service poetry, ragtime music, and can-can girls. It was a most enjoyable and hilarious show. Soapy was reincarnated by a superb actor. He made us keep our hands on our wallets and purses.

At Scagway, we boarded a small overland train called the White Pass and Yukon Route Railway and travelled along the picturesque white pass trail to Whitehorse in the Yukon Territory. Whitehorse is the Yukon's capital, with a population of 28,000 arctic-seasoned souls. Few cities in the world offer such access to pristine wilderness yet provide modern amenities. The town is hugged by the banks of the Yukon River and surrounded by the peaks of Grey and Golden Horn Mountains. It was a hub for transportation and logistics during the gold rush. Gold seeking stampeders travelled down the Yukon River and crossed the White Horse rapids form which Whitehorse got its name. This was a dangerous and treacherous operation at best, and many didn't make it. Supplies and equipment were seen daily floating down the river along with frequent bodies of the unfortunates who had been dashed against the rocks with their make-shift boats in the roiling rapids.

Unique attractions in Whitehorse include the Yukon Quest, an annual international dog-sled race, in February, that runs between Whitehorse and Fairbanks, Alaska. The mushers with their teams will arrive in 10 to 16 days. One musher told us that "unless you were the lead dog in the team, the view was always the same." The race is growing in popularity and some say it will soon overtake the Iditarod the famous Alaskan race run from Fairbanks to "Florida" one of our group offered, but I think he was kidding.

The Yukon Sourdough Rendezvous Festival also run in February features axe throwing, dog-sledding, chainsaw chucking and flour packing (I don't know what that is, but it sounds flowery?). Over the same period, the International Snow Sculpting Challenge draws carvers from around the world who create stunning snow sculptures along the waterfront. In June they have a canoe and Kayak race along the local waterways.

For family entertainment the Frantic Follies, a vaudeville revue is celebrating 48 years of laughter in 2017. Not far away to the NW is Muktuk, not Mukluk, (I looked it up) Adventures providing sled-dog experiences for all ages. Whitehorse, like all other gold-rush boom towns, was also famous for their many saloons with gambling and ladies with painted faces who relieved the miners of any money they had remaining with what one guide called "negotiable affection and passionate participation."

Who said there was nothing to do in the North? Surely, not the Northerners.

Another claim to fame in Whitehorse is that Pierre Berton, the author of *Klondike* lived there, that's Pierre Berton, not Richard Burton, in case you were wondering. A lady in our group who had a southern drawl and a huge hearing aid like a doorknob, asked if "they were related." Our guide was speechless; she just shook her head.

We motored next by bus from Whitehorse to Dawson City, still in the Yukon. As a lark, I sat in the back of the bus next to the washroom (restroom as our guide called it; come to think of it some people were in there for quite a while—maybe they were having a nap). I started charging a quarter to use the washroom/restroom, that's 25 cents Canadian and 20 cents American. In the nine-hour trip, I made a buck and a half, (1.20 American, I think). I would have made a lot more if I charged for the toilet paper, but I didn't think about it until later.

After the discovery of gold in the area, miners on the scene staked claims to every tributary creek to the Klondike River they could find. Not until mid-1897 did the outside world learn of the strike when some of the newly rich prospectors arrived by steamboat at Seattle. The headline in Seattle's Post Intelligencer description "of a ton of gold, worth millions" triggered a veritable stampede to the Klondike gold fields. Another Texan (a rancher, I believe) recounted that "they used to have e stampedes with their steers when they move them up North to the meat packing plants in Chicago."

"Good to know," our long-suffering guide returned.

It is said that one million people laid plans to go to the Klondike, a hundred thousand set off and about 30,000 made it. One of the obstacles was the insistence by the famous head of the NWMP, (North West Mounted Police) a precursor to the RCMP, Sam Steele, that gold seekers heading to the Canadian Klondike in 1898 must carry goods to survive for a year over the Chilkoot Pass. A list of supplies included 400 pounds of flour, 100 pounds of beans, and 100 pounds of sugar. The average man took 40 trips to haul his ton of supplies 33 miles over the Chilcot Pass. That was a total of 2,600 miles over exhausting icy trails, up the Pass (the golden stairs) at the summit, going through blizzards and sub-zero temperatures. It took at least three months of drudgery to make it to the gold fields. Most either died or turned back. What was a native fish camp and moose pasture for many generations was transformed into a striving metropolis over the space of two years. Once the Yukon River thawed in May of 1898, hundreds of mostly make-shift boats arrived each day in search of the elusive mother lode. For a time, Dawson was the largest city north of Seattle and west of Winnipeg. This set off the Texan again. He related that Texas had the biggest steaks, the biggest oil wells and the biggest land mass in the United States." After being corrected by a local guide, about the land mass, he said with the sibilance of a whisper, that "Alaska might be a little bit bigger."

In Dawson, we visited the cabins where famous authors Robert Service and Jack London lived. They both lived very spartanly and were renowned for their unique descriptions of people's and places in the Far North. Robert Service was poor in his early career and was reputed to having taken long strides to save shoe leather. He is also recorded as saying "[d]on't let grammar get in the way of a good rhyme, and "[r]ebuttals are just rungs in the ladder of success."

The Cremation of Sam McGee and the *Shooting of Dan McGrew* are two of his most popular and widely read poems. Jack London is most celebrated for his *Call of the Wild* and *White Fang.*

Another world-famous gimmick in Dawson is the sour toe cocktail. A drink, alcoholic of course, is offered (for a price of course) with gray-coloured amputated toe in it. The owner of Dirty Gertie's Saloon swears that it's a real toe cut off from one of the many frostbite casualties in the area every winter. For just five bucks you can line up at Dirty Gertie's (If Dirty Gertie was in Whitehouse, she could have bought some soap from Soapy Smith, she might not have been so dirty") and prepare for some almost-cannibalism. Next with your purchased drink of Yukon Whiskey, the 'Toe Barman' as he's called, ceremoniously slips the grey toe into your glass with a flourish and you drink it down like a shooter. However, swallowing the toe is forbidden; the fine is now 2500.00 a hand-made sign below the toe bar read—I wondered how they collected said fine, as well as how they get the toe back. Toilet vigil, perhaps?

A patron who obviously frequents the place often (his stool was molded in the shape of his butt) told me, in a sort of a whisper, that they had many spare toes in waiting in the freezer out back. He said they got them from the local medical centre called "the chop shop." He said that he often wondered if the toes really needed to be amputated or were they cut off to refurbish the toe supply. I think the medics got paid for each toe.

Good work if you can get it.

I asked if the big toe cost more than the rest; He didn't know for sure but said he would find out and tell me the next time he saw me at Dirty Gertie's. He told me, confidentially, he could get me one for a good price, $100.00 or $80 .00 American. I politely declined. "I've still got my own toes," I told him. I also made a private vow not to get passed-out drunk in Dawson.

Our guide also told us there is often a long line up and you can wait an hour before getting your chance. They call it a toe jamb.

A short fat guy, wearing a red plaid lumberjack's shirt, with about 14 teeth missing, bewhiskered with a long scraggly beard, and a tussle of flaxen hair, gave us more valuable information. He was called 'armpit with eyes' the barman told me, by his friends—I hate to think what his enemies called him. He told us in a low gravelly whisky voice that "Yukon Whiskey is very strong and harsh, (I could tell how he knew that), but it's the only stuff that prevents 'toe main poisoning.'" A warning worth remembering.

It was also in Dawson City that I saw my first large wild animal—a Sasquatch. We were told, confidentially by one of the locals that 4000 people went missing in Alaska every year without a trace; the elusive Sasquatches were suspected of eating them. We kept a close vigil, especially at night for these, some would say, mythical creatures. We walked tentatively, in groups of four, checking out the gathering shadows, and listening intently for any strange noises (like howling or growling) to prevent attack by these fierce creatures.

Later that night, I ventured outside my room, into a dark hallway, at our rustic hotel to try to get a glimpse of the Northern Lights, scientifically named the Aurora Borealis. I saw a shadowy figure of a large unkempt, hairy creature shuffling along sort of bent over. I froze, terrified, as the apparition came close to me and into the dim light. I was preparing to bolt or be eaten, but to my great surprise and relief, the creature was my brother looking for the bathroom. When he saw me cowering outside my door, and I squeaked "I thought you were a Sasquatch," he began to laugh uproariously, at my expense, and he told everyone he met about my near-death experience that night. But, I got him back the a few days later at breakfast.

"After all," I recounted to anyone within earshot, "My brother is quite hairy, weighs over 300 pounds, he walks with a bit of a shuffle and he had his shirt off; anybody could have mistaken him for a sasquatch."

"Before I travel with him again, especially up here, he has to get a shave and a haircut and wax his back!"

That night, well after midnight, we also got to see the spectacular performance of the dancing, dazzling Northern Lights. The lights, colours and movements burst onto the night sky and turned the darkness into a magical light extravaganza in all its ancient glory.

The midnight sun waned under a pewter sky, on the horizon, at first, like a pre-dawn glow, it then becomes a great plume of filigree across the heavens. A small, scrawny, professorial looking man with a goatee beard and thick coke-bottle glasses gave us a scientific commentary of what we were looking at. "The auroras run the full spectrum of colours depending on the composition of the earth's atmosphere at the time" he said. "Red auroras are created from high altitude oxygen, while green is by oxygen at low level. Nitrogen in the atmosphere causes blue or purple auroras." We were treated to most of these hues along with fire-like embers shooting out in all directions to frame the brilliant sheets of light. It was a rather perfect climax to our short stay in Dawson. We left the next morning.

From Dawson City, we bussed our way to Denali National Park, the largest wildlife preserve in Alaska, not to mention Mount McKinley, now Mount Denali, the highest peak in North America and according to our bus driver, the highest peak in the world if above sea level is considered. Eat your heart out, Mount Everest. They have sasquatches in Nepal too; they call them Yeti. So, the shave-haircut-wax-back rule applies to my brother for any trips to Nepal as well.

At Denali, we saw many large animals including moose, (swamp donkeys as they call them in Alaska) deer, wolves, caribou, mountain sheep black bears and grizzly bears. We were constantly warned not to feed the animals or go near them, especially moose ('Don't moose with me', was one sign we saw) and grizzly bears (no warning necessary). Our guide told us that if a moose charges you, you're supposed to run in a zig zag pattern to confuse them—because they can't see too well, (I'm not making this up). If you are attacked by a black bear, average of about 200 pounds, you fight them off. But grizzlies are another story. If attacked you lie on your stomach, in the fetal position, with your hands behind your neck and play dead. It's good practise for what's likely to follow.

This might be a bit difficult if the bear is chewing your ears off. At least you wouldn't hear the chewing and slashing. Have you all seen *the Revenant*?

Our guide also told us that he sold bear whistles, which, when blown loudly and continuously, could scare bears off. He said they were scientifically invented at MIT. I think they also made mitts, to produce an audio frequency that irritates the ears of the grizzly. He mentioned, as an added feature, that the whistles could also be recycled.

A lady from Connecticut asked how that was possible.

"Oh", said the guide with a straight face, "we pick the whistles out of the bear shit and sell them to someone else!"

A friend of mine who lives in the lower 48, gave me an alternate method for fending off a grizzly before I left the safety of the southern climes.

"When he comes within twenty-five or thirty feet throw a rock or stick at him," he said, "try to aim for the nose. At fifteen feet get out your bear spray and spray him in the eyes. When he gets within five feet, throw some shit in his face."

"But where do I get the shit from," I asked innocently. He looked off in the distance to compose himself, and then sagely whispered, "Oh you'll have some."

Another technique mentioned by a fellow traveller was "to outrun the slowest man/woman." There were several people with walkers on the bus, so I felt more secure. I could outrun at least one of them.

Next, we took a much more elaborate train from Denali to Fairbanks, also in Alaska. When we stopped for lunch, the restaurants were full, so we went to a street vendor selling hot dogs and bratwurst. The sign read 'our hot dogs are hot, and our bratwurst are brat best.' A New Yorker mentioned that they called this stuff "street meat." He asked me what we called it in Canada.

"Roadkill," I said.

The same lady from Texas overheard this and told me that they had a problem with wild hogs in her state. "They're everywhere," she said, "we've got over three million of them; and they're dangerous with their great big tusks like butcher knives!"

"Do you have any wild hogs in Ontario?" she asked.

"No", I said, "but we do have sabre toothed squirrels."

She had a sort of puzzled look on her face and said, 'Oh, Really?"

"Yes,' I said, "You don't want to run into one of them, they're real ugly." I think she believed me.

The Iditarod, the famous 2000-mile dog-sled race, starts in Fairbanks. I noticed several dog sled parking spots in the area. The signs read "Dog-sled parking spot—Violators will be peed on."

Across the road a homeowner with a well kept, almost manicured front lawn, had a sign in gothic print; It read "Here they lie cold and hard; the last dogs that shit on my yard."

We next took another train to Anchorage, the major city in Alaska with over 350,000 people and two massive military bases for both the US Army and US Air Force. Staying in the Sheraton Hotel, we got to talk to many of the locals and read about the area. Our bus driver told us that Alaska had the highest addiction rate and suicide rate in the US, mostly due to the prolonged darkness and isolation. We asked him what he does in the winter.

"Drink," he said. "Same as most people."

He went on to say that "it's dark for nine months and light for just three. So, you can get away with a lot in the winter and you have three months to apologize in the summer, when they can see you." Good plan.

The next day, after a bowl of reindeer chili, we flew back to Vancouver. I asked our waitress, a cute little girl from Thailand named Sara, what was the difference between reindeer and caribou?"

"Reindeer fly," she said, with not a hint of an accent.

We left the land of the Midnight Sun after two weeks. We had learned that the denizens of the North were the most innovative, friendly and talented people on the planet. Although, very few have made any fortunes. These citizens of the snow are delightful to visit. They thrive on the many challenges of this frozen wasteland; shared suffering and isolation keeps them together.

The trip was a blast, as my young grandson would say. Now, when we feel a cold gust from the north on our face or look up to see the North Star, we will think fondly of our odyssey to the magical 'Land of the Midnight Sun.'

The people we met were hardy survivors.

ACKNOWLEDGEMENTS

My inspiration for this work came from myriad sources. To my loving, long-suffering wife Maureen, who has been enduring my tales for almost twenty years, and laughed out loud at the good, chuckled politely at the bad and winced quietly at the ugly; I am forever in arrears.

To my seven siblings Marie, Dave, Jane, Steve, Phyllis, Nancy and Ben, who listened to my incessant jokes and stories for at least six decades, sometimes laughing and sometimes groaning,

I owe a great debt.

To my hundreds of in-laws and outlaws (over 400 at last count) who gave me the models for my characters, I am much obliged.

And finally, last but not least, my writing group, The Scribes of Northumberland (The SoNs), from Campbellford Ontario; Mary Lou, Mary Jane, Martha, Marie, and Jackie, and sometimes Art and Wendy who listened intently to my ramblings and gave me honest valuable criticism, I salute you for your talents and thank you for all your help in this endeavour.

About the Author

Lieutenant-Colonel (Retired) W.A. (Bill) Leavey served in the Canadian Army Infantry from 1967 to 2008. The field units he served in include the Black Watch, Royal Highland Regiment of Canada (RHC), the Royal Canadian Regiment (RCR), the Canadian Airborne Regiment (CAR), and the Princess of Wales Own Regiment (PWOR). From 1994 to 1998 he was seconded with Veterans Affairs Canada as military liaison officer for the Canada Remembers Program, a commemoration group celebrating battle and campaign anniversaries for all of Canada's major wartime events. Bill holds a master's degree in English from the Royal Military College. He has written two books of anecdotes for the RHC and RCR, entitled *War Stories, Anecdotes and Lies*. Bill has also published numerous stories, articles, and essays on military humour and humour in general in local and national magazines and newspapers. In the past two years Bill has written essays for Volumes I, II, and III of Lammi Publishing's *Canadians and War* series. He lives in Kingston, Ontario with his wife Maureen, a 35-year veteran herself, and their mini-Australian Labradoodle (part Kangaroo), Finnigan.

Bill travelled the world during his military service to such exotic places as Burma, Thailand, Cyprus, much of Europe, Israel, Lebanon, all the provinces and territories of Canada, and many US states and learned much from the people he encountered. He often commented that he "never met a person yet who couldn't tell him something he didn't know."

About Lammi Publishing Inc.

Incorporated in 2014, Lammi Publishing is dedicated to publishing Canadian military history from the wars before confederation to the mission in Afghanistan. Our philosophy is that we cannot forget. Our mission is to be a method of remembrance. Canadian military history has shaped not only our politics and government, but our society as well. Canadians naturally take pride in our famous victories in Western Europe, Afghanistan and South Africa. From the oceans to the air, Canadians have done their duty with skill and valor. Peacekeeping operations have taken our forces far and wide bringing hope and security to so many. Canadian uniforms have been seen around the world as harbingers of liberation, from Belgium in WWI to the Netherlands in WWII to Yugoslavia in the 1990's.

It is only by having easy access to material on these events that we can understand them, put them in context and remember. Information, analysis, and the memoires of those who served should be readily available instead of being locked away in a desk or a long forgotten bookcase in the back of a library.

The rise of electronic books means that it is now possible for anyone to easily compile a library that would rival the best that our public libraries or universities can offer, with no more worries about short print runs and the vagaries of the antiquarian market.

To learn more about us and what we are doing,
check out our website.

http://lammipublishing.ca

Lammi
Publishing Inc.

CPSIA information can be obtained
at www.ICGtesting.com
Printed in the USA
LVHW011443011219
639013LV00016B/432/P

9 781988 932101